IRT

SURGEON FROM THE USA

When Sister Patty Henden meets a handsome American tourist, the attraction is mutual. Neither realizes at first that they are both in the medical profession. Dane, however, has to leave next day on a one-year European lecture tour. Communication between committed surgeon and busy nurse is difficult as Dane moves from place to place, and Patty begins to feel that the relationship is doomed. The last straw is hearing that Dane has an American girl-friend . . .

IRENE SAMSON

◆

SURGEON FROM THE USA

Complete and Unabridged

LINFORD
Leicester

First published in Great Britain in 1990 by
Robert Hale Limited
London

First Linford Edition
published 2000
by arrangement with
Robert Hale Limited
London

British Library CIP Data

Samson, Irene
Surgeon from the USA.—Large print ed.—
Linford romance library
1. Love stories
2. Large type books
I. Title
823.9'14 [F]

ISBN 0–7089–5765–X

Published by
F. A. Thorpe (Publishing)
Anstey, Leicestershire

Set by Words & Graphics Ltd.
Anstey, Leicestershire
Printed and bound in Great Britain by
T. J. International Ltd., Padstow, Cornwall

This book is printed on acid-free paper

To
Sam and our brood,
with special thanks to Mandy

1

'Sister Henden, please come — the man in the second bed is haemorrhaging!' . . . 'Sister Henden! Two patients are being sent up right away from casualty!' . . . 'Sister, the CNO's in the dutyroom!' . . .

Patty Henden awoke with a cry, and the feeling familiar to all hospital nurses, that someone on their ward needs them urgently. She sat up in agitation, and found herself in her pink bedroom at home, the sun streaming through the open curtains. Her heart was racing, and it was several moments before the near-panic of the jumbled dreams seeped away, leaving her blissfully aware that she was on week-end leave, and that almost two full gloriously unprogrammed days lay before her.

'Come in!' she called in answer to a

light tap on the door, and her mother tiptoed in with a cup of tea.

'Wasn't sure if you'd be awake so early,' Mrs Henden said. 'You looked so exhausted last night. I know it takes you ages to unwind.' She sat down on the side of the bed.

'Thanks, Mum.' Patty took the cup gratefully. 'This week's been hectic. I was dreaming of something — can't remember what it was now, but thank goodness it was only a dream. I've had enough real emergencies for the moment. The phone rings non-stop, and if it isn't casualty, it's theatre. We've been so busy, I thought I might have to stay on, but Staff Nurse Barry's super — efficient and conscientious — and she's good with the patients and the staff as well. I'm lucky to have her.'

'And I should think she feels lucky to have you.' Mrs Henden smiled fondly at her only daughter. 'The gale last night didn't disturb you, I gather?'

'Was there a gale? Didn't hear a thing.'

'It seems to have done a great deal of damage in this part of the country: roofs ripped off, chimney stacks blown over, trees . . . one of the big branches of the apple tree came down.'

'Not the one the swing hung from?'

'The very one. I expect it had been weakened over the years. Gerry often sits on it when he's reading, and he's no featherweight.'

'What a shame!' Patty thought affectionately of being pushed higher and higher by her father until her head touched the upper branches; pleasure tinged with apprehension Gerry had fallen off it once and broken his arm.

'Have you any plans for today?'

Patty finished her tea and put the cup on the bedside table. 'Nothing in particular. That's what's so lovely about coming home — no commitments, no clock-watching. I've one or two things on my mind, though; might use some of the time to think about them; never seem to get the chance to think in hospital.'

'Ah,' said her mother. 'I guess you'll be off on your own this morning, then. To your usual haunt. I shall do the shopping, and see you at lunchtime. Have you arranged to meet Eric?'

'I haven't phoned him. He doesn't know I'm home. May just leave it like that.'

Her mother looked at her questioningly, but said only, 'Breakfast in about fifteen minutes, if you feel like getting up. Or would you like the royal treatment — breakfast in bed?'

Patty, now wide awake and eager to make the most of the day, shook her head. 'Not really, thanks, Mum. I'll have a quick shower and go down.'

Ten minutes later she was towelling herself vigorously, rubbing as much wetness as she could out of her hair — it would dry in the warm air of the house. It was heavenly to dress at leisure, in casual clothes; she used a body spray of her favourite perfume liberally, and pulled on a pink and

4

green striped top and pale pink trousers.

A slender five feet five inches, she appreciated her good luck in being able to maintain her weight, no matter what she ate. Her ash-blonde hair fell to her shoulders; she wore it in a chignon on duty. Her mother's oval face and her father's hazel eyes made a cool, aloof impression on strangers, hiding the essential warmth within.

She looked out at the garden before she left the room and saw the severed limb of the old tree lying forlornly on the grass, the ancient swing caught underneath. Mr Henden had left early for golf to avoid the week-end queues, and only her brother Gerry was at the table when she went downstairs.

'Hi,' he said, his mouth full of cereal.

'Hi.' She smiled. 'Working up a hate for the opposition?' Gerry never missed his rugby game on a Saturday morning, even if it was only a friendly during the off-season, as now.

He nodded, swallowed what was in

his mouth. 'Don't know if hate will be enough, though. They beat us twenty-five — nil the last time we played them. The only good thing is that we're playing at home, and our brave handful of supporters is ready to shout down their supporters and hopefully demoralise the team. Don't suppose you'd care to lend your voice to the chorus?'

'Sorry, Gerry. I've planned a quiet weekend.'

'Been having a hard time?' The gap between their ages had been a barrier while they were young, but now they had an adult understanding of each other's lives that Patty treasured, cemented on his side since he'd started his PE course, and his eyes, the same hazel as hers, were genuinely concerned.

She shrugged. 'No more so than usual, I suppose. I think I'm a fraction less tolerant when the weather's good outside the ward and I'm stuck inside.'

Mrs Henden brought eggs and toast for the three of them, and they chatted desultorily until Gerry rushed off, leaving the two women alone.

Patty Henden was wrestling with a problem, though no one but her mother would have suspected that anything untoward was going on behind the tranquil front she presented to the world. The give-away was the location she'd chosen for the struggle — a municipal art gallery and museum.

Patty was no artist; she had a minimal interest in sculpture and ancient pottery and thought old tapestries were simply dust collectors, however painstakingly worked. It was heresy for a person like her to frequent Farnton's latest repository of such treasures, she admitted to herself, and yet, from her first, tentative visit, the Shearton Gallery had become for her a refuge from her job in general and the hassle on Ward Eight, men's surgical, in particular.

Only a half-hour's walk from her suburban home, the gallery called for no dedication or formality, and she often spent a morning or an afternoon there when she was home, invariably returning with a more equable view of life. She was hoping today's outing would do something in the way of solving her dilemma.

Breakfast over, Patty brushed her hair up into a ponytail and anchored it with two combs, pocketed her house keys, took enough money for a cup of coffee, and set out.

Like all her friends, she'd been taken by her parents during her schooldays to the city's concert halls and theatres, museums and art galleries — 'hoping something would stick', Mrs Henden had remarked only recently, during a nostalgic look into the past.

The expeditions had given Patty and her brother pleasant enough memories, but Gerry was now studying to be a physical training instructor, and she'd become a nurse. He had a lofty scorn of 'culture vultures', and Patty seldom mentioned her visits to the gallery.

The wealthy industrialist who had

bequeathed the accumulation of a lifetime's collecting to the city had stipulated that it should be housed in a pollution-free environment, and a short, brisk walk brought Patty through suburban roads and into the huge Linton Park that had become the home of the gallery.

On the way, she'd noticed with dismay the trail of destruction left by the gale — ruined gardens, roofless garages. Here the damage was even more shocking. A number of trees had been blown down, and lay, fallen giants, their great roots exposed. Such devastation seemed incongruous in the gentle sunshine of the morning. One tree that had blocked the roadway, was being dragged aside by a huge tractor, leaves and twigs lying in its wake.

Patty quickened her step. The unusual, angular Shearton building was in sight, nestling into a semicircle of woodland, a vast expanse of grass spread before it. She reached the arched doorway, and stepped into the cool, austere reception area, consciously cleared her mind of its muddle, and relaxed.

The gallery attracted visitors from all over the world, and a small crowd had gathered beside a notice-board that announced that the next guided tour would leave from there at 10 a.m.

On an impulse, Patty attached herself to the fringe and looked casually round at her companions: several elderly people in a group of their own, chatting together; some Japanese men, hung with cameras; sun-tanned couples, probably on holiday; unattached young people, sex almost indistinguishable in the standard T-shirts and faded jeans.

The tour was scheduled to take an hour and a quarter; she'd stay with it for about half the time, then wander off. She'd developed a fondness for some of the Impressionist paintings, and would sit and look at them later, then perhaps go up to the mezzanine floor and admire the wonderfully fine embroidery.

A middle-aged woman strode purposefully towards them. 'Mrs Wirral,
Official Guide,' was the inscription on
the badge pinned to her cardigan. She
had the severe look of the teacher, hair
drawn back into a bun, heavy spec-
tacles, and held a sheaf of documents.
When she reached them, she smiled,
and the severity disappeared. She
introduced herself, and the visitors
instinctively moulded themselves into
an entity.

'Good morning! How nice to see
you all!' She made it seem as if they'd
come to visit her and she was about to
offer the hospitality of her home. 'Are
any of you on holiday?' Most members
of the group raised their hands. 'How
lovely! Anyone from abroad?' Half
appeared to have come from the
Continent, the Far East or America.
'Delightful!' Mrs Wirral exclaimed, as
if she meant it, as if she hadn't
conducted the same monologue at
least once every day of the past two
years. The gracious hostess changed

subtly back to the schoolmistress.

'Now, this gallery was built in . . . '
Patty knew the story, every citizen of
Farnton knew it, and she listened
absently, letting her eyes take in her
surroundings, following the lines of the
building, enjoying the soft warm tones
of the sandstone arches that led to
different parts of the collection, each
one rescued from some crumbling old
castle and integrated into the architec-
tural scheme.

From where she stood she could see
part of the courtyard that had been
designed as a setting for an enormous
marble vase, elaborately carved, which
had once graced the garden of a Roman
emperor. She couldn't see the vase, but
her angle of vision took in two bronze
life-sized figures standing among the
trees which had been planted shrub-
high and now reached the high glazed
roof.

The origins of the gallery had been
dealt with and they were moving on.
Patty, at the back of the group, had

noticed one young couple, apparently two long-haired boys, but now firmly identifiable as boy and girl, walking close together, fingers interlocked. The visual screen that was her memory switched to Eric.

A GP, practising in her home town, he'd come to her ward in Westingham General to visit one of his patients, hospitalised outside his own area after being injured in a road accident. He was persistent about making a date with her. Young and personable, he had the further merit of being unattached to her hospital — she'd always had a horror of being a news item on the hospital grapevine — and eventually she'd relented. They had a meal and went to a cinema on one of her nights off, and had fallen into the habit of going out during one or other of her week-ends at home.

It was all very casual, which encouraged Patty to keep seeing him; she wanted no serious entanglements right now. Conversation revolved round

Eric's world, and she was quite content to listen to his interminable complaints about high authorities and criticisms of diagnoses at consultancy level. His good-night kisses caused no flutters of her heart. So she was quite unprepared, the night they'd gone out of town to try out a country pub, when Eric observed, over the coffee, 'I think you and I should get married!'

She'd laughed, treating the remark as one of his rather ponderous jokes. 'Right! How about next Wednesday? I'm off from two to five!'

He wasn't amused. 'I'm serious,' he frowned. 'I think we're very well suited, Patty. We speak the same language and you understand the pressures of my job. You could be a big help to me. Look, I've been planning. We could buy a house big enough to have a surgery attached, and you could be my surgery nurse — it would only be for a couple of hours a day, morning and evening, or afternoon — we could make times to suit both of us.'

Patty stared. It was certainly no joke. He had it all worked out. Belatedly she realised that he'd taken her acceptance of his invitations as a commitment to something far more binding. She saw her role in his life with dismay. 'And the receptionist duties — appointments, filing, paperwork?' she stammered.

'That wouldn't be any more than you have to do as a sister, surely? And you'd be at home, remember that. No more responsibility for all those patients, dealing with emergencies, kowtowing to the doctors, putting up with stupid juniors, night duty.'

'You mean, give up nursing altogether?' she said flatly.

'Patty, you don't want to stay on at the hospital until you're all dried up and dehumanised like the CNO, do you? You're young and warm and healthy; don't you want a husband? And babies? Your biological clock's ticking away. Don't tell me you're one of those ghastly libbers who'd like to see a world without any men at all?'

It had been a disturbing exchange. Disturbing in that it had probed a very sensitive area of Patty's soul. Only recently she'd met up with a friend who'd gone into district nursing . . . Sheila . . .

Patty was finding it difficult to concentrate on what Mrs Wirral was saying, as they went from one glass case to another looking at Egyptian relics. The guide's words faded away as Sheila's earnest voice took over. She'd been the Sister on the ward when Patty was staff nurse, and they'd become very close. Patty remembered the heart-searching before her friend left the hospital.

'I don't want to graduate into administration,' she'd said, talking it out with Patty. 'Nursing's what I always wanted to do, and I don't intend to do it by remote control. I've been a sister now for three years and it's time to move on. Working on the district seems to be the next logical step; for me, anyhow.'

Sheila had married her boy-friend, and was now working part-time and planning their second baby — the first was already a self-possessed toddler attending a playgroup. 'When you're on the district you see folk as they really are, the whole picture: environment, financial circumstances, family, from babies to old people. You always looked on your patients as people, not simply occupants of this or that bed, didn't you, Patty? That's one of the things that makes you a good nurse.

'What's specially nice is that as a district nurse you're somebody to your patients, a real person, coming into their homes, not just another figure in uniform. Being married, with kids, of course, gives the job an extra dimension.

'Today's district nurse is an extension of the hospital service — patients are discharged as quickly as possible, as you well know, on account of the shortage of beds, and who do you think carries on where the hospital leaves off? Think about it, Patty.'

Patty had thought, long and hard. Was she in danger of getting into a groove? Administration had no attraction for her, either. Sheila had highlighted another niggling worry, and Eric had aggravated it. It was unthinkable that she should never have children. Weeks on the maternity unit — an experience that put some nurses off the idea of pregnancy — had strengthened her determination that one day, in the not too far distant future, she'd be handed her own baby carefully into her arms, the way she'd so often settled someone else's precious new-born son or daughter; and, of course, there would be a dearly loved husband in the background . . . Eric?

The group straggled down the corridor, and Mrs Wirral embarked on a review of the fragments of ancient stained glass, set into the windows, which spilled rainbows on the floor . . .

Sheila had it all, the husband, the family, the work she loved. Love didn't appear to come into Eric's plans. Mentally Patty reviewed this young man who was causing her such introspection. Passable as far as looks were concerned: reddish-brown hair, brown eyes, small moustache. He looked clean and honest, fitted in well with her family — her father discussed golf with him, and he seemed interested in Gerry's wide-ranging sporting activities; her mother approved of him.

She couldn't help feeling, however, that he saw her only as cheap labour, her reward lying in being rescued from a dubious future by his brand of knight in shining armour, and supplied with a couple of babies to keep her happy. He lacked something: sympathy? warmth? Could she tell him about her arrangement with Gerry? Would he understand?

He'd probably make a good enough husband — so long as she rearranged her life to suit him. Perhaps she'd be glad to do just that . . . if he didn't take everything for granted . . . if he even once said 'I love you' . . . if she loved him . . .

And what is love, anyway? she mused as Mrs Wirral pointed out a man and a woman closely entwined on a pedestal among the bronzes. Unlike most of the other girls in her set, she'd refused all invitations from the medical students when she was a student herself, and, later, from the housemen and junior doctors. 'Ice maiden', she'd been told, was the nickname she'd acquired as a Sister, and she'd once overheard one doctor comment to another, 'The only way to get to Patty is by breaking a leg on her ward and having to be kept there as a patient!'

For the last two years she'd deliberately avoided all male involvement, as part of her self-imposed plan, and now agonised, finding it impossible to cut herself off from Eric, continuing to see him when they had the same evenings free, and to play for time in answering his proposal. I am healthy and young — fairly young, she told herself, and I certainly don't want to finish up like Miss Brendrith . . .

The script was smooth. 'Now that you've had a taste of the very old pieces that Mr Shearton collected, you'll appreciate the range of exhibits as we move to more modern works in the painting gallery,' Mrs Wirral said, making a neat link in the story, then, as she spotted a colleague striding through an archway with a line of acolytes struggling to keep up with her, realised that schedules had clashed.

'Sorry, I must have taken too long over Greece,' she apologised, pink with embarrassment. 'The Fine Arts tour has got ahead of us. Let's take a look at the Elizabethan Room at this point.' Her group smiled sympathetically, entirely on her side.

Patty took one look at the ornate throne 'specially built for a visit of Elizabeth One. Our queen was very interested in this when she visited the gallery,' and decided she'd had enough. Waiting until the guide was looking the other way — it was surely something of an insult to abandon the tour mid-lecture — she drifted out into another corridor and made for the painting of the Virgin that always gave her pleasure.

'All through?' An American voice at her shoulder made her jump. One of the anonymous young men in the group had followed her. She'd noticed him join the tour some time during the visit to the ceramics.

Patty flushed guiltily.

'I know how you feel,' he went on, without waiting for an answer. 'I can take so much culture, and no more, and that Elizabethan stuff was the last straw.'

She smiled at his frank admission. 'I live locally so I often come along,' she explained. 'That was the first time I've joined a tour, though, and I feel rather ashamed about walking away from it, but I think I prefer to be on my own.'

'You're an expert, then, I take it?' Topping her by about six inches, he was browned by a lot more sun than he could possibly have found in Britain; his hair was bleached by it; blue eyes crinkled at the outsides as if he smiled often. He smiled now, and his teeth were American — as white as his shirt and almost artificially regular. The quintessential Californian, she guessed.

'Don't know a thing,' she confessed, warming to him. 'I come here to relax. Sounds peculiar, perhaps, but I find something here — it seems to put my little problems into their proper perspective. Nothing seems to matter quite so much when I leave here.'

They'd reached her Virgin, and she stopped. 'I love this one,' she murmured, prepared for him to make a jokey comment.

He studied it, stepped back, looked at her. 'Guess you could have been the model,' he observed, and she felt her face redden once more. 'The same shape of face, the very expression of — of serenity.' He took her by the shoulders and held her away from him, his head on one side. 'You're very

23

beautiful,' he said dispassionately. 'If I were a painter I'd kidnap you and bring you back to my studio and keep you prisoner until I'd painted you at least a thousand times!'

His eyes were piercing, almost magnetic, and she stared up into them as if she were mesmerised, sweet sensations she hardly recognised flowing through her from his touch, her heart thumping. If he'd kissed her at that moment, she would have melted against him, and when he released her, almost abruptly, she felt somehow cheated.

'Gee, I'm sorry about that,' he said. 'Say, let me take you for a cup of coffee to make up, OK?'

She nodded, shaken. He'd felt something, too. Neither Eric nor any other man she'd dated had ever begun to arouse her the way this stranger had done. It was dangerous. Coffee, and no more, she vowed, leading the way to the cafeteria.

They sat opposite each other at one

of the long pine tables, a vista of grassy slopes and distant trees beyond the windows, and he had no difficulty in finding conversation. Dane Culver, he introduced himself, 'of CA — California, that is — trying to see everything worth seeing in as short a time as possible.'

'I'm in the Shearton, it must be Saturday,' she slipped in, and he threw his head back and laughed.

'Not quite like that. My itinerary's actually been pretty flexible. I've had some leeway to extend my stay here and there, but there is a limit.'

He told her about his home — 'on a hill; that's fairly mandatory over there. Without the ocean breeze it would be unbearably hot most of the time. We have a good percentage of sunshine. Haar rises from the ocean on spring and summer mornings — a shivery phenomenon — and doesn't vanish until the sun's hot enough to burn it up. And we actually get some rain in the winter, and, occasionally, a little frost. Brrr!' He shivered melodramatically.

'But if you like flowers?' She was hanging on his every word, and nodded, smiling. ' — then we have them all — bougainvillaea, hibiscus, lilies, jacarandas . . . Nothing like this greenness, though — ' He indicated the lawns outside.

'What about earthquakes?' Patty asked innocently.

'Ah, yes. We try to forget about those. They're not normally more than faint tremors. But frightening none the less. The snakes in the Garden of Eden, you might call them.' His eyes were on her, and she was swept by an illogical and out of character desire to be held close and kissed, and hurriedly looked away. He was probably married, with children back in the States; he looked over 30.

'I have to be in London tomorrow. That leaves this afternoon and evening . . . Patty, take pity on a foreigner adrift in a strange land, will you, please?

Unattached and lonely. Come out with me?'

'How unattached?' She despised herself for asking, but she had to know.

'Over here? No attachments, ma'am. I'm free as a bird. Back in LA — Los Angeles — one ex-wife, one son of four, David by name. Look — ' He pulled out a wallet and extracted a snap of a small fair-haired boy poised to dive into a swimming-pool.

'He's sweet,' Patty murmured.

'Guess so. Shaping up well at swimming — all the kids are water babies back home — and making a good show at pre-school basketball.' He spoke with pride. 'He's a busy young-ster.'

'You miss him?'

'Sure do. Call him every night when I'm home. Miss that. He's a good kid. Now, about this afternoon. How're you fixed? I'm staying at the Milton Hotel in the centre of town. Where do you live? I have a hire car, may I pick you up, at, say, three? You can show me some of the sights I've missed and suggest a decent eating place — do you eat Indian, Patty? I've acquired a taste for curry since I've been over.'

She didn't hesitate. 'Love it. And, thanks, I'd enjoy going out with you.' It sounded prissy and old-fashioned, but Dane beamed as if she'd given him a longed-for gift.

She refused his offer of a lift home, but couldn't dissuade him from walking out into the park with her 'for a last look round'. A signpost indicated 'The Rose Walk' and he said, 'Let's look at the roses, Patty, before you go, and see if they're as good as ours.' It was a challenge she was happy to accept.

They set off along a path lined with rhododendrons, pink and crimson and purple, rising some ten feet high and creating an illusion of privacy. He took her hand, and held it lightly.

'Are you at college, Patty?' It was the first personal question he'd asked, and she laughed.

'Heavens, no! I'm well past college age.'

'No kidding — if you'll excuse the pun? Hey — the way you wear you hair, your clothes — you don't look more than sixteen, but I thought, perhaps eighteen!'

'Regret to disillusion you. I'm all of twenty-five.'

'I don't believe it! And to think I was afraid I might be cradle-snatching! Are you single? Do you work? Or are you a married housewife with a brood of kids? Or any permutation of the three?'

'I'm single, I work for a living and I have no children.'

He stopped, his face unsmiling, put his arms around her and drew her close. 'Dear Patty, I've gotten quite fond of you in this short time. May I kiss you — if you're sure you're over sixteen!'

She lifted her face to him, and when their lips met she felt great joy surging through her. The flowers exuded a cloying scent around them. He smelt of after-shave, his lips tasted of coffee. When he let her go, she staggered, light-headed and off-balance.

'My dear girl, what are you doing to me?' He took out a handkerchief and wiped his brow. 'Patty — I don't know quite what to say. Sorry to have forced myself on you; glad you're you! Can you beat it, I come on a culture tour and find a dream girl!'

Patty was fighting to cling to the last shreds of reason. 'The rose walk is farther on,' she pointed out.

'Yes, yes,' he said distractedly. 'The rose walk. I'd forgotten about the rose walk.'

She was very conscious of the warmth of his arm lying across her shoulders as they rounded a bend, and felt a glow of pride in being able to show this visitor from a country of flowers, the glorious spread. Almost every colour of the spectrum was represented there, perfume filled the air, and from the bees working around the blooms came a faint, continuous hum.

'Wonderful!' Dane breathed, stooping to sniff at an exquisite deep red rose, a dewdrop still shimmering on its petals. Patty's gaze moved idly beyond the flower border to where an uprooted tree lay among a clump of shrubs, a violent intrusion in this idyllic place. Luckily, the roses were spared, she was thinking, when a patch of blue tangled in the fallen branches caught her eye. It shouldn't be there. She frowned, caught her breath, and ran, heedless of the thorns that ripped at her trousers. She heard Dane's startled, 'Hey, where — ? What — ?' Then, as he saw where she was headed, 'God!'

Everything was driven from her mind and years of training took over as she knelt beside a small child lying still and silent on his back, eyes closed, legs pinned down by one of the smaller branches of the tree. She'd turned his head to the side and was feeling for a pulse when Dane reached them, expertly lifted an eyelid, and listened to his chest.

'Slow beat, no internal bleeding,' Patty muttered. 'Possible concussion and leg fractures.'

'Snap!' Dane said, and they looked at each other in sudden awareness.

'You're a doctor?' Patty said.

'I am indeed. Try to keep incognito when I'm on vacation, for obvious reasons.' He was lifting the branch as he spoke, and she stood up to give him extra leverage in breaking it off. 'You, too?'

'Nurse.' This was not the time to swop career histories. The child lay sprawled, one foot ominously twisted. He was wearing blue pyjamas and one muddy slipper with a rabbit on it. The other lay nearby. He didn't look more than three. 'His pyjamas aren't wet, he can't have been here long,' she observed. 'Not through the night, anyway, the dew would have soaked them.'

Dane was running his hands over the

little form. 'Go call an ambulance, Patty. And the cops — his parents must be frantic. I'll try and make him more comfortable.'

He replaced the second slipper, and as Patty ran off she saw him unbutton his shirt and wrap it round the child.

When she'd made her calls, Patty alerted the security staff on duty at the doors of the gallery and asked them to direct the ambulance down to the rose walk. Dane had improvised splints, using branches secured with the belt of his trousers, and was lying in the undergrowth alongside the boy to give him warmth from his body. His chest and back were as tanned as his face and arms.

'Don't ask me to stand up,' he grinned. 'You may get an eyeful of rather *risqué* undergarments if I forget to hold my pants up!'

Glad to see him happy enough about the boy's condition to make a joke, Patty knelt down on the other side of the child and stroked his cold cheek lightly. The eyes flew open. 'Hello,' she said.

Dane sat up eagerly. 'Hi, what's your name? Mine's Dane. Guess you came out for a walk in the woods before breakfast? You must be real hungry!'

'Daddy,' a small voice quavered. 'Daddy!' Lips trembled, big brown eyes filled up with tears.

'Hey, you're not going to cry, a big guy like you?' The wail of the ambulance could be heard in the distance. 'Listen, an ambulance! Have you ever had a ride in an ambulance?'

The boy shook his head, tears momentarily forgotten.

'The siren makes such a noise, all the other cars on the road stop to let it go by. And the ambulance is coming out here specially to give you a ride! How about that?'

They were suddenly surrounded by men in uniform. The boy grabbed hold of Dane's hand and stared in terror.

'Here's the driver of the ambulance,' Dane told him. 'He's going to drive

34

very fast indeed. And here's the cop who's going to tell your Mommy where you are so that she can come and see you.'

He disengaged the little hand and within minutes the makeshift splints had been replaced by more orthodox ones, and the boy, covered with blankets, was being carried on a stretcher to the open van. 'Daddy!' he screamed, trying to catch Dane's hand again.

'May I come along?' Dane asked. 'I'm not his father but I'm a doctor. I may be able to keep him calm. He'll be hurting real bad soon.'

The two ambulancemen looked at each other. 'O.K. Go ahead.'

Dane climbed inside, pulling his shirt on, suddenly remembered Patty and looked back anxiously.

She waved him away. 'See you later,' she called, as the ambulance went forward towards a clearing where it turned, then set off on its noisy way to the nearest casualty department.

The police officer was speaking on a walkie-talkie, listened, then spoke some more. 'We have a report of a missing child,' he said. 'Sounds like our wee fellow. We'll get the parents up to the hospital right away.'

Patty picked up a little blue slipper. It had fallen off again. She handed it to the policeman and he put it in his pocket.

2

Patty's thoughts, as she walked home, formed ever-changing pictures of Dane. The real man, she thought, was seen in those few moments when the child had recovered consciousness. He was the kind of doctor who gave everything to his patients, who put them even before his family. He'd actually forgotten I was there, she reflected. Perhaps that's what went wrong with his marriage. It would take a very special wife always to stand aside and give way; but he was a very special man.

She changed when she arrived home, before her mother noticed her stained and torn trousers. Mrs Henden was preparing lunch. 'Have a pleasant morning, dear?'

'Yes, thanks.' Patty couldn't divulge her crazy, mixed-up feelings even to her.

'Good. You usually feel refreshed after you've been to the Shearton. Probably the sight of all those old, old things. They make you realise how trivial our lives are, don't they? Stop you worrying — for the time being — then, of course, it all comes back again. But that's life, isn't it?

'You have a stressful job, and you'd need to be as hard as stone not to be affected by it. And I know your feelings are as susceptible now as when you were a student and came home in tears after dealing with all those frightful cases. Remember?'

She was waffling on, to give Patty the chance to recover from whatever had made her so unaccustomedly terse; Patty knew that. She and her mother were on the same wavelength. She couldn't go on keeping from her one of the most incredible experiences of her life. Gerry and her father would soon be home and the opportunity would be lost.

'Mum.'

'Yes, dear?'

'Mum, I met someone at the gallery.'

'You did?' She paused. 'Do you want to tell me about — er — him, or her?'

'It was a him — a he. An American. He's doing a tour of Britain.'

'How interesting. What part of America does he come from?'

'California.'

Mrs Henden was busy at the cooker.

'The thing is, I'm going out with him today.'

'Oh, that's nice.'

'He's coming here to collect me. I'd like you to meet him — if you're not going to be out.'

'Of course I'm not going out. I always try to keep my week-ends free when you're due home. I'd love to meet him. Shall I count him in for dinner?'

'I'm going to show him around the town in the afternoon — he's hired a car — and he wants to have an Indian meal tonight.'

'Good choice. Ah, here's your dad.'

'Don't say anything to him or Gerry,

please, Mum, they'd only jump to conclusions.'

'Of course I won't.'

Patty felt self-consciously that the family must see some difference in her, some outward evidence of an inward radiance, as she tried to show an interest in Gerry's explanations of his team's second unlucky defeat, and her father's triumphant round of golf. She felt more the age Dane thought her than the age she was; more like an adolescent in the throes of first love than a balanced, self-confident ward sister.

The two men went out immediately after lunch to a football match, Gerry, broad and tall, towering over his rather stocky father, so Patty had no explaining to do to them. Her mother would say casually that she had a date, when the evening mealtime approached; they'd assume it was with Eric.

Patty dressed with care, in a lime-green sleeveless dress that emphasised her slimness and made her eyes look greener than they were, and white sandals with high, slender heels. She loosened her hair and brushed it until it shone, and used the minimum of make-up, carefully lining and shading what she considered her only good feature — her eyes. It was no sacrifice to go without make-up on duty, she detested having her face layered with beauty preparations.

'How do I look?' she asked her mother, as she had over the years, from her first dates as a gawky, nervous schoolgirl.

'You look a knock-out! Easily a match for any Californian glamour girl!'

'That's the whole idea, naturally! Mustn't let us Brits down. Seriously, Mum, OK?'

'Lovely. Borrow my white jacket, it may be chilly later in the evening.'

She was ready long before Dane was due, her hands cold and clammy with a mixture of excitement and trepidation. Supposing he's had second thoughts, she worried; supposing he's already on his way to London. Perhaps he's married and doesn't want to spoil things for himself by saying so. Have I made far too much of a kiss, made a fool of myself over a casual encounter with a stranger?

He was there, at last, standing in the doorway. He'd changed from white shirt and denims to a pale blue silky roll-neck sweater and light blue trousers, and his eyes seemed more startlingly blue than before. He looked down on her for a long, grave moment, without saying a word, and folded her into his arms. She nestled against him, almost unbearable longings flooding through her. Letting her go, he tilted her chin up with one finger.

'Yes, you sure do look like that Madonna, honey. Thought my memory might be playing tricks. But here you are, beautiful and hot-blooded and alive — while she, poor dear, hangs with her baby on the cold dead wall!'

He tucked a hand under her arm as

she led the way into the room where her mother was innocently reading a newspaper. She watched Mrs Henden beam as Dane held out his hand and said, 'Glad to meet Patty's Mom,' and went to collect her jacket.

'He's charming,' Mrs Henden confirmed in a whisper as Patty turned back at the door to say goodbye. 'And you look charming, too.' Raising her voice so that Dane could hear, she called, 'Have fun, both of you!'

Afterwards, Patty tried to recall any fun they might have shared, but her memories were overlaid with sadness. From the time she buckled her seat belt in the hired car, she felt constraint between them. He squeezed her hand, leaned over and kissed her on the cheek before they set out, but it was as if he were distancing himself from her.

'Saw our little friend nicely settled in the children's ward,' he said with satisfaction, as they drew out on to the main road. 'Waited around until he'd been X-rayed. No skull fracture, thank goodness. Fracture of right foot; the other leg's only bruised. Mom and Pop were brought along by the cops and a tearful reunion took place, but he's tucked up now with his teddy, and the nurses are spoiling him already.' He was as pleased as could be, Patty could see. 'And, by the way, no wonder his muddled little brain mistook me for Daddy — we're quite alike!

'They found the rabbit hutch open, worked out that he must have gone into the garden to play with Fluffy and then followed her when she ran off. They live just outside the boundaries of the park, and it was easy enough for the little fellow to scramble through the wire fence. The tree was probably poised, just ready to fall. A lucky escape, really. Full marks to you, Patty, for being so observant; he might have been trapped there for much longer.

'Incidentally, I specialise in spinal surgery, Patty. You a hospital Sister? Guess you're too competent to be anything less.'

Patty quietly confirmed it.

'So let's skip talking shop — OK by you?'

He concentrated after that on driving to her directions, carefully watching for one-way streets and the jay walkers the city was notorious for, but was content to gaze from the car at the famous buildings she pointed out. Sensing he was merely being polite, she soon lost interest, too, and guided him to the river where walkways stretched along both banks, lined with flowers and shrubs.

They left the car and strolled slowly along beside the shining water. The traffic noise receded to a distant hum, small birds darted from bush to bush, and a field mouse scuttled from the shelter of the undergrowth, spotted them, and fled back again.

Dane put an arm round Patty's shoulders, and began to speak slowly, choosing his words. 'Good to be with you,' he said 'you have a quality of peace about you, and God knows I need some. Maria, my ex-wife, left me two years ago. I found work took some of the pain away, and I've never stopped since. I've felt worse about the whole sordid business during this vacation than I felt at the time; some delayed reaction, I guess.'

They came to a wooden bench and Dane drew her down beside him.

'It seems a lifetime since I started at med school. Had to study hard to stay there, and take jobs — anything — during vacations to pay my way. The habit of overworking stuck. Maria didn't understand — how could she, she'd never spoken to a doctor before she met me, not even for a consultation. She couldn't see that we can't function on a nine to-five basis, can't walk away from a human being in pain, can't refuse to treat an emergency even if we happen to be at a fancy ball when the hospital calls.' He sighed, and Patty took his hand and held it.

'Oh, I missed her, Patty, don't think I didn't. I loved her. All in the past tense, of course. I couldn't fight her for custody of David; that was the worst part. He was only two at the time, what kind of home could I provide for him, with hired help all the way? What a mess!

'Get to see him plenty, I've no complaints about that, and I'm hoping to fix it for him to visit with me over here during the year I'm away. There are usually personnel coming and going who could bring him. Got to be satisfied with that . . . '

He was so silent, and both remained so still as she waited for him to go on, that a grey squirrel flashed along the path, inches from their feet, oblivious to them.

'Patty, I guess I came on pretty strong yesterday.'

She shivered involuntarily, and his grip on her tightened.

'I didn't mean to let you know how I felt. It's not fair to you.'

He's engaged to be married, she said to herself; he's getting married when he goes back. Or she's going to join him over here.

'That divorce tore me up, Patty. I'm not ready to take on another relationship. I'd be no good at it . . . And there's something else — '

They both watched a small motor boat putt-putting up the river, cleaving the still water, leaving a line of ripples in its wake that spread out wider and wider until they slapped against the walls under the walkway on each side. It was the only human intrusion since they'd stopped at that quiet point.

'When I said I was on vacation, that was perfectly true. The vacation finishes tomorrow. On Monday I start on a lecture tour, in Europe and the UK. It's going to take a full year, because I'm staying on in a number of teaching hospitals to demonstrate several techniques I've pioneered.' He sighed.

'My dear little English rose,' he said huskily, caressing her hair and tracing the line of her cheek. She flushed at his touch. 'Rose with pink velvet petals . . . Patty, I'm not naïve enough to expect you to wait for me on the strength of our ridiculously short acquaintanceship, but I shan't forget you. I'll find you before I go home, that's a promise.'

They ate their curries in a shadowy restaurant where the only lighting came from red candles in red glass holders on each table, and lingered over coffee, but the finality of the evening clouded any enjoyment she might have felt.

She watched him speak, memorising the way his hair curled over his ears, noting the golden eyelashes glimmering in the candlelight, the glint of his splendid teeth, the gestures of his hands, with their long, tapering fingers; the hands of a surgeon, some might say, though she'd seen the finest, most delicate work done in theatre by hands that looked too large and clumsy to hold a needle.

He refused her invitation to come into her home for a final drink, and kissed her goodbye in the car, a tender, affectionate kiss that left her with an inexpressible feeling of melancholy. She couldn't face her family when she went in, and looked round the door to apologise, saying she was tired and was going straight to bed. She ignored her mother's concerned look.

Next day was dull, matching her mood. Mrs Henden tactfully made no mention of the night before, for which Patty was grateful, but when Mr Henden was settled with the Sunday papers and Gerry had gone out to meet a friend, Patty wandered into the kitchen where her mother was baking.

'Coffee?' Mrs Henden enquired, and switched on the electric kettle. Patty collected three mugs and brought one in to her father before settling back in the kitchen, now redolent with the smells of apple pie and coffee.

'What did you think of Dane?' She felt a compulsion to talk about him.

'It's not easy to form an opinion of someone who says only, 'Glad to meet Patty's Mom' and 'Goodbye, Mrs

Henden, glad to have met you,' but he's so handsome — that Californian tan! — and he acts like a gentleman. But you don't need me to make a character assessment, surely? You've enough experience yourself of judging people . . . Something upset you last night, dear, didn't it?'

Patty felt like the small girl she used to be, crying to her mother about trifles that seemed all-important at the time, and tried to hold back; her mother couldn't work the miracles for her now that she performed years ago. But the mother-can-fix-everything tradition was too strong.

'Mum, I hardly know him, but I love him.' Her voice shook and treacherous tears threatened. She gulped down some of her coffee to help her pull herself together.

'Did he say he loves you?' Mrs Henden's concern showed in her eyes.

'No. But I know he does. But he's gone abroad — on a year's lecture tour. He said it wouldn't be fair to ask me to wait for him, but I would have waited if he'd asked. I don't think I'll ever see him again — and I feel an absolute wimp crying on your shoulder like this! I'm a complete idiot, behaving like a soppy kid. Heavens, what would the CNO think if she could see Sister Henden in such a flap!'

'Fortunately I'm not Miss Brendrith,' Mrs Henden said bracingly. 'Come on, Patty, you know tears are of no help, and you'll have me as depressed as yourself at this rate! Here — I'll give you a job to do, manual labour's the best thing for making you forget your sorrows. Prepare these vegetables for me, and make sure the leeks are properly cleaned!'

Patty smiled tearfully at the old admonition — she'd always hated brushing the grit out of the tightly rolled leaves of leeks, and often tried to get away with a quick wash. After a moment or two she was sufficiently composed to bring her mother up to date with hospital news.

'Jackie's fixed her wedding for Christmas and she's applying for a month's leave of absence so that they can go over to Canada for their honeymoon and make the rounds of Ken's relatives.' Ken was a junior medical registrar at Westingham.

Mrs Henden was pleased. She knew Sister Jackie Christie well. She'd been a frequent week-end visitor during the years she and Patty had trained together. 'So she's decided to continue nursing when she's married?'

'So she says. Ken's quite agreeable, but I can't see it working out. Think of their shifts — I can imagine the assistant CNO deliberately putting Jackie on nights when she knows Ken's on days, and vice versa. She disapproves of married couples working in the same hospital.'

The telephone rang, and Mrs Henden nodded to Patty to answer it. Patty's heart had jumped; perhaps Dane had cancelled his departure to London? It was Eric.

53

'Is that you, Patty?' He was surprised. 'I didn't know you were off this week-end. Why didn't you let me know? I was calling to ask your mother if you were coming home next week.'

'I — er, I was awfully tired. We've had an exceptionally heavy week — ' No point in going into details; Eric was interested only in himself.

'Oh, I see,' he said doubtfully. 'Well, have you a free evening next week?'

'Next week?' Mrs Henden, making a shrewd guess at Eric's question, was nodding vigorously. 'Well, yes, I should be off at five on Thursday if no emergencies show up.'

'Good. I'll push off early and go through in time to pick you up at seven p.m. All right?'

'Er — fine. I'll phone if I have to cancel. Thanks.' She replaced the receiver and sat down heavily. 'Mum, what am I doing? I don't want to go on seeing Eric, yet something compels me. And do you know what it is? I'm getting older, and I want to be married and have a home of my own — and a baby, before it's too late. And I don't want to marry Eric.'

'My dear, no one can help you with a decision like that. But if you have the slightest doubt, then wait. Rushing into marriage is the worst thing a girl can do. If you really don't want Eric, then say goodbye to him on Thursday, because if you have doubts about him now, they won't go away when the ring is on your finger.'

'You're right, Mum, as usual. I'd been worrying about this before Dane turned up. Now I'm sure. I won't marry Eric and be his nurse/receptionist or anything else he dreams up, and I'm not going to mope over Dane, so don't worry about me. Someone else will materialise out of the blue, you see if I'm not right. Everything will work out — that's what you used to tell me when my world had fallen apart! Thanks!' She hugged her mother and they clung together affectionately for a moment.

'I haven't done a thing,' Mrs Henden

said. 'You worried it out for yourself before you spoke to me. And I know you won't have time to fret once you're back on duty, so I'm not going to have any sleepless nights over you. And, for goodness' sake, don't brood over your age. You've got years in hand before you're too old to have a baby!'

Mrs Henden was right in one respect: there was no time on a busy surgical ward for romantic schoolgirl fantasies or love-sick yearnings. On the following morning, Patty took over the night report with single-minded attention and gave Staff Nurse Barry her orders. The night staff had prepared three patients for theatre that afternoon; an emergency of the day before was still being carefully watched; and one of the juniors was on a week's leave.

Patty had trained at the Westingham General, and graduated to staff nurse there. When Sister Baynes of Ward Eight had finally given in to her husband's plea and left to settle down on their farm and start a family, Patty was elated to be offered the post. The elation had given way to quiet satisfaction in running an efficient ward, helping to train the next waves of student nurses, finding more and more fulfilment in doing the work for which she'd trained so long.

As a Sister she had a far more rounded view of each case, though she often missed providing the essentially personal care the nurses gave, and occasionally found an excuse to give a blanket bath or massage an aching back, ostensibly 'to keep my hand in', in truth, to have a chance of speaking to the individual patient and getting a deeper insight into the person than the case notes revealed.

She started her ward round unhurriedly. Staff had organised the students, now busy on their routine work, and the trolleys were being set for the medicines and dressings.

Over the week-end there had been changes. The new face, belonging to the previous day's emergency, was pale but cheerful under its turban of bandages. The 'morning, Nurse', was a trifle slurred, which was no surprise coming from a young man who'd been struck on the head and knifed in the abdomen. X-rays had shown no fracture, but he was in the bed nearest the door where Patty could keep an eye on him from the dutyroom window and no one going in and out could miss him.

Patty forbore to correct his 'nurse'. He'd soon learn the staff rankings. 'Does your head ache?' she asked, consulting his chart. Temperature, pulse and respiration were all slightly raised.

'Sure does.' He spoke carefully; obviously the slightest move caused him pain. 'And my tum. Otherwise I'm fine.'

'Hang on.' She patted his shoulder. 'Nurse will soon be round with the medicines.'

'Ta, Nurse.'

Patty heard the hiss as she moved away from the bed, as one of the up-patients whispered to him, 'Sister, mate! She's the Sister!'

Last week's splenectomy, an elderly man who was allowed up in the afternoon, wanted to know if he could get up now, as there was a programme he wanted to see on the television in the dayroom — the ward TV was never on before lunch. He was advised to wait until after the doctor's visit. It was good to see him showing an interest, Patty thought, remembering his fear of surgery when he was brought in.

The three theatre cases, already in their white operation smocks and woollen socks, were trying to outdo each other in bravado. 'Hi, Sister, we're still waiting for breakfast! Thought the condemned men were to get a hearty meal before the execution!'

'I've changed my mind, Sister — I don't fancy the show that's running this week!'

'I can see I'll have to order some extra jags — looks like that'll be the only way to shut you up!' Patty was joking. She had a good mix of patients just now and it helped everyone if someone poked fun at the system now and then.

Even the old man whose colostomy operation was looming up had no complaints. She'd spent a lot of time with him, explaining the operation and what to expect after it, and was pleased to find him calm and mentally prepared. 'Only three days to C-Day,' he said, 'and it can't come quickly enough.'

'You'll have a new lease of life after they take away the bad bits,' she reassured him.

'Aye, I reckon so.'

Nurse Henry, the third-year student, accompanied by the first-year, Nurse Thomson, wheeled in the medicine trolley as Patty reached the last bed, and she found Nurse Barry in the corridor with the dressings trolley. 'Let me know when you're starting Mr McLeod,' Patty said, going into the dutyroom. The rather dour Scot had been brought back in after an amputation when the stump began showing signs of infection, and Patty wanted to take a look before the surgical registrar made his round.

She made a note of a few questions for Mr Simpson and went over the case histories to make sure they were up to date. The medicine trolley rattled back from the ward and Nurse Henry knocked to ask permission to replace some of the mixtures and tablets in the poison cupboard. The junior came up to say Staff Nurse Barry was about to start Mr McLeod's dressing, and by the time she came back the students were setting beds and lockers to rights before the visit.

Patty felt a pleasant sense of anticipation as the outer doors of the ward swung open and shut and footsteps approached. She'd been dismayed when Mr Simpson was appointed less than three months before, replacing dear old Mr Sullivan who had retired after being at Westingham 'boy and man' and was the most popular member of the medical staff.

Tall, painfully thin and ascetically severe in looks and expression, the new senior surgical registrar gave his orders in a tone of voice that suggested he hadn't much hope of their being carried out. Patty found herself reacting with an abruptness that had its roots in nervousness. She was unhappy that the relationship between the two people most important to the ward should be so fraught, but didn't know what to do about it.

The breakthrough was unexpected. Patty, worried about a post-operative case that she thought was beginning to haemorrhage, called Dr Dykes, the junior doctor, who proved to have an afternoon off. She made up her mind not to wait, and got in touch with Mr Simpson direct.

Prepared to be ticked off for daring to bring him to the ward unnecessarily, she was surprised when he gravely returned with her to the dutyroom after examining the patient, and congratulated her on her vigilance in nothing the danger signals, telling her that he wanted the man in theatre at once for a repair. His grey eyes, usually icy, were soft, and the first smile he'd ever produced on her ward, flashed out like a ray of sunshine.

Thereafter, when there was no full-scale teaching round, the ritual coffee break previously taken after the visit in a chilling silence, became a congenial ten minutes of surprisingly irrelevant chat. Patty slowly found the deeply sensitive man behind the cold image, learned of the hurt caused by the death of his wife five years before, and began to understand why the protective shell had been erected.

Her friend, Jackie Christie, on women's surgical, had agreed with Patty's first diagnosis. 'Yes, he's a cold fish. Fine with the patients, but appears to despise all sisters. Must have had a bad one at sometime or another and puts us all into the same category.' She was amazed to find Patty buying chocolate biscuits to go with his coffee.

Patty mentioned briefly to Jackie that Mr Simpson had lived alone since his wife's death rather than move to a hospital residence, and had a morbid dread of some woman taking advantage of his situation. Since the women he met most often were on the hospital staff, it followed that he looked on ward and theatre nurses with suspicion. She seemed to have gained his trust, but was careful not to relax in his company, always deferring to him, fearful of seeing the shutters go down again and those all-seeing eyes freeze over.

'Good morning, Sister.'

'Good morning, sir.'

'Any problems?'

Patty had her list ready, mentioned several patients she wanted guidance on, and they went into the ward, which was impeccably tidy and unnaturally quiet. Staff had done her usual dependable job.

Mr Simpson came to life at each bed,

addressing each patient by name, encouraging them to tell him exactly how they felt, making his examinations with sensitive fingers, then resumed his mantle of remoteness towards his retinue. Doctor Dykes hung on his every word, Patty handed him each case history in turn and noted every instruction, Staff Nurse Barry, bringing up the rear, picked up the folders of the patients who had been seen. It was an efficient, if somewhat cowed, team.

After the round, Doctor Dykes sped off on other business. Cursed with an inferiority complex, he had no confidence in himself, and tried to avoid situations in which his professional knowledge might be called to account. Patty waited until the surgeon was seated at her desk, then took the other chair, and the junior brought in the coffee tray. Patty saw Mr Simpson's eyes turn to the biscuits, and a gleam appear.

'Chocolate chip cookies?' he wanted to know.

'We call them 'Mum's biscuits', sir, my brother and I.' Mrs Henden had insisted on her taking a tinful back to the hospital with her. 'Give your poor hard-working staff a change from shop biscuits,' she said.

He appeared not to have heard her. 'Chocolate chip cookies,' he repeated, breaking off a crisp piece and crunching it. 'Perfect,' he pronounced. 'My wife was American, you know. She used to turn out trays of these. Your mother made them, you say? Is she American, too?'

'No sir. She's been producing these since my brother and I were children. Please help yourself — ' The first one was already gone.

'They're very good. I wonder where your mother picked up the recipe.'

'I doubt if she has one. She's one of those cooks who makes up her own recipes as she goes along, and probably evolved it by accident by her 'a pinch of this and a handful of that' method. I'll ask her to make an extra batch next time I'm home and bring you some.'

'Thank you, Sister, I'd appreciate that.' He drained his cup, inclined his head as Patty offered the coffee pot for a refill, and took a third biscuit. 'Thank you. I've two wards still to visit, and a heavy theatre list for the afternoon, which starts at one p.m., so I expect I'll miss lunch.'

Patty frowned. 'Have you time to wait until my junior produces a couple of slices of toast and butter, sir? It would be more substantial than biscuits.'

'Considerate of you, Sister, but I shall refuse your kind offer. I frequently go without lunch. I shall have a good dinner tonight to make up.' He looked thoughtfully at her, and she blushed faintly under his keen eyes. 'I suppose — I wonder — er, would it be possible for you to join me? Er — of course, you're most probably already er — er — ?'

Despite her astonishment, Patty was touched by the spectacle of the great man bereft of words, and, mindful of the blow to his frail ego if she refused, stepped in to save him. 'Thank you, sir, I should like that, I'm off at five tonight, so any time after that would be convenient.'

He looked relieved. 'Thank you, Sister. Say, seven p.m.? I look forward to that.' He put his cup down and stood up, ready to relapse once more into the impersonal. He'd forgotten to fix a meeting place. Patty thought quickly. She didn't particularly want the entire nursing staff to witness the assignation.

'May I suggest that I meet you outside the side gate, sir?'

He grasped the significance at once. 'Yes, yes, of course, Sister. I hadn't thought . . . '

'Thank you, sir.' She opened the door for him, stood aside to let him go out first, and accompanied him up the corridor, as protocol demanded. His face had set into its customary auster-ity, but she hugged to herself the knowledge that he was definitely human after all.

Back in the ward, the radio was on, providing a background of pop music, up-patients, in dressing-gowns were on their feet, the bed patients had already ruined the precise angles of their sheets as they read the morning papers or wrote letters, the junior was doing her back rubs.

Patty sat down at her desk and wondered how she could have let Dane Culver vanish from her mind so quickly. Two days ago she'd been in a fever of desire for him; today she'd already made a date with someone else, and on Thursday would be seeing Eric.

Nurse Barry knocked to collect the case histories of two patients going up for X-ray, and the physiotherapist, Jane Anston, checked in before starting her work on the ward. Patty reminded Staff to do the three pre-meds, and looked out their X-rays. Drawing a deep breath, she smiled to herself. She felt young and vibrant and in command of her life. 'Everything's going to work out,' she said aloud, echoing her mother's frequent assurances, but, with the prescience painfully acquired along the way since those early days, she prudently crossed her fingers as she spoke.

3

Patty had complete faith and trust in Sister Jackie Christie. The two had shared a room at the preliminary training school, and confided in each other ever since. They'd vetted each other's boy-friends, and taken each other's advice, and even now, with Jackie making active plans for her marriage and spending every possible minute with Ken, they were as close as ever.

Yet they looked an unlikely duo. Jackie's dark curly hair and brown eyes contrasted with Patty's fairness, and she had often tried new and short-lived diets in an effort to reduce her rather stumpy figure to Patty's proportions. In a moment of desperate comparison, she had once declared that her friend 'wafted along like a cloud of Chanel', a description that Patty often recalled with an inner chuckle when she was in the midst of some especially insalubrious situation.

Like the lounge at the residence, the Sisters' area of the dining-hall was a centre of gossip, and they tried to avoid listening to the character assassinations and wild rumours that were aired there. Many potential romances had been wrecked by the spread of inaccurate reports. Patty was wary of being seen speaking to a doctor outside the ward; the one sighting would be enough for malicious embroidery to be added on as the story was passed from mouth to mouth. Jackie had been a focus of attention when she first met Ken, as someone who 'knew' insisted that he was already married. It took an engagement ring to hush up that one.

So Patty instinctively lowered her voice as she joined her friend for lunch. Jackie had already finished her soup and she was devoting her attention to cold meat and salad when Patty put her soup and roll on the table.

'The most unbelievable thing has happened,' she whispered.

Jackie looked up with interest. 'The CNO's got engaged? The Chief's getting a divorce? They're going to marry each other?'

'Even more improbable. I'm going out tonight for a meal with Mr Simpson!'

'What?' Jackie almost choked, coughed, and had to swallow half a glassful of water. 'I don't believe this! You dark horse, you, how did you manipulate this situation? With chocolate biscuits?'

'Ssh,' Patty begged, looking around them warily. 'You know what the gossips can do. I'm meeting him at seven outside the side gate.'

'Cloak and dagger stuff, eh? Well, I'm not sure what to wish you — if 'good luck' is the right blessing. You know what I think of our Mr S.'

'Good luck doesn't come into it, honestly. I think he asked me on the spur of the moment and is probably regretting it right now. But he's not such a bad old stick, and I just couldn't refuse.'

'Oh, don't I know that kind heart of yours! The lame-dog syndrome — you've obviously applied it to that wretched man. Just don't get into anything heavy, Pat. He may be a raving Casanova behind that glacial exterior! Maybe he murdered his wife and dismembered her body — that would be child's play for him! A nice change from his theatre work — no anaesthetic to bother about!'

Patty giggled. 'Jackie, do stop! I'm going to laugh now every time I see him.'

'I mean it, Pat. I'm glad you told me you were going — he won't be able to act the innocent if you don't come back! Well, you know I mean it for the best, don't you? My advice is for your own good. Don't look too alluring — the change from uniform might drive him mad with lust!'

The two parted to go back on duty,

Patty wiping tears of laughter from her eyes. She hadn't mentioned Dane when she saw Jackie the previous evening, determined to forget the incident. This diversion would help to take her mind off him.

*   *   *

The afternoon passed without complications, and Patty left the staff nurse in charge for the evening shift with a clear conscience, going back to the Sisters' home to have a long, hot bath, and read for an hour before she dressed for dinner.

Mindful of Jackie's advice, she looked through her wardrobe, and decided that none of the clothes she kept at the hospital could possibly be classed as alluring. For her occasional dates with Eric, she kept several summery skirts and a selection of tops, and now chose a yellow skirt printed with ears of wheat, with a deep border of royal blue cornflowers and scarlet poppies.

A lemon blouse seemed appropriate; pretty but unrevealing.

Dane hovered at the back of her mind, and she was suddenly overcome with longing that he was the one she was about to meet. No use thinking that way, she was going to spend some time with Mr Simpson — she didn't even know his name — and how that was going to turn out was anyone's guess. She hoped the evening wouldn't spoil their future standing on the ward, and resolved to tread carefully.

His car was waiting when she left the hospital, and she smiled to him as she stepped in, sensing his head-to-toe inspection. He drove away fast and competently, and she realised the car was a powerful sports model.

'You're punctual, Sister,' he said. 'No trouble in getting away?'

'No, sir. I have a very good staff nurse. I've every confidence in her.'

'Ah yes. Being able to trust a colleague is essential . . . Please don't call me 'sir', Sister. When I leave the hospital I try to leave my professional image behind. My name is Ronald — Ronnie, usually. Yours?'

'Patricia. Best known as Patty.' He was wearing a sports jacket and open-necked checked shirt. Ronald. Ronnie. Funny how a name changes one's perception of a person, she mused. He now looked like any other youngish man at leisure. Thin, yes; facial bones very prominent. But that might be from neglecting mealtimes.

'I do hope you will forgive my not taking you to a restaurant,' he said. 'The invitation was given on impulse — ill-mannered of me, I know, not to give you some notice — and I'm taking you to my home to eat. I have a housekeeper who is an excellent cook, and she's been warned — if that's the right word! — to expect you.'

'Sounds good,' Patty said sincerely, suppressing a suspicion that the chaperone would depart after serving the meal; bother Jackie and her imagination! 'It's easier to wind down at home than in a public place, and I'm sure your day's been frantic, as usual.'

'Yours, too, I expect. I do agree with you that eating at home is more restful, and I hope you enjoy the experience of eating in mine. As you know, I live out, for personal reasons. Mrs MacTaggart looks after me beautifully. She's Scottish, which may account for her care of me — and I'll leave it to you to form your own judgement of her culinary capabilities.'

They left the town and took the road for the coast, turning off the motorway at a lonely stretch of moorland and following a slow winding road to a small village she recognised from being taken there with Gerry as children by their parents for a picnic by the sea. Mr Simpson drove smoothly between two opened gates into a carriageway and up a slight slope, to a small but picturesque cottage. Manicured lawns on each side of the drive were edged with clumps of colourful flowers, and from the front door the rocky coast and sea were in full view.

'How lovely,' Patty breathed, getting out of the car. The house seemed much larger inside than the exterior suggested, white walls probably adding to the illusion. There were flowers everywhere. A small, stout, white-haired woman bustled into the hall, presumably from the kitchen, for she had a huge white apron wrapped round her.

'It's yourself, Mr Simpson, and on time for once!' Her tone was tart.

He looked ruefully at Patty. 'This is my housekeeper, Mrs MacTaggart. Miss Henden.'

'How do you do, Mrs MacTaggart!' Patty extended what she hoped was the hand of friendship, and was relieved when the woman shook it warmly, her face softening into kindliness.

'I'm right glad to see you, m'dear. You're both looking tired, so away you go through and sit down until I'm ready to serve. Give your friend a drink, Mr Simpson. You'll not be taking spirits yourself if you're to be driving her home.'

They looked at each other and laughed when they went into the lounge, and his face was almost happy. 'She bullies me something dreadful,' he said, 'but she's a wonderful person. I'd best give you a drink or I'll be in for a telling-off, and in front of you, too. So, what will you have?'

Patty settled for tomato juice, and walked over to the window with her glass. 'What a marvellous spot!' The sun was setting, and the sky blazed with shades of orange and purple. The sea was bronze. 'It's so peaceful. Well off the beaten track, yet handy for the hospital.'

'Yes, that's why I chose it. I feel I'm in a different world here. A world without ghosts.'

She nodded, understanding the reference. The room was comfortably furnished, and had several ceramic and crystal ornaments, unpretentious but pleasing. More flowers were massed in bowls on the window ledge and on small tables. She sank into an armchair and sighed contentedly. 'So many flowers! From your garden?'

He was standing looking down at her. 'My hobby is gardening. It gives me great pleasure. Only snag, I have to wear gloves to protect my hands — and scrub up in theatre twice as long as anyone else!' He sat down at last, and stretched his long legs out in front of him.

'Do you manage any sort of private life — Patty?'

'Not in hospital. That would be impossible. Read a little. See the occasional film. Avoid television. Walk — with Sister Christie whenever we're off duty at the same time. You know her, of course — Ward Fifteen.'

'Yes, I know Sister Christie.'

'We started our training together and have been friends ever since. She's getting married at Christmas. To Doctor Sylvester. I suppose you've heard?'

'Well, no. I don't seem to hear about such things, though I know there must be a grapevine, every hospital has one. I work, I come home — a rather solitary life, but I like it that way.'

'I like to get away on my own, too; usually when I have problems.'

'What sort of problems?'

He was more interested than inquisitive, Patty knew, but she had no intention of exposing her soul. 'Problems that seem world-shattering at the time and utterly trivial when I look back on them afterwards,' she said lightly, and Mrs MacTaggart came in to say dinner was ready.

The housekeeper, who gave the impression that her cooking would be as robust as herself, surprisingly produced a meal of simple delicacy. They started with avocado, went on to the main dish of salmon — 'Scotch, Miss Henden,' the cook pointed out — with an assortment of salads and tiny buttered potatoes, and finished with a light spongy strawberry gâteau. 'My own baking, Miss Henden; none of those frozen things for me — you never know when they were made, do you, or what's in them?'

Mr Simpson poured a sparkling white wine into crystal glasses, and they had coffee at a small table in the window alcove and watched the evening sky darken to navy, and the first stars sparkle out.

Conversation had been superficial, and Patty felt comfortable in his company. 'That was a delicious meal,' she said. 'Now I understand why you don't mind missing lunch! I'd never eat in the hospital either if I had cooking like that to come home to.'

'I'm glad you enjoyed it.' He paused. Patty waited, staring out into the darkness. He had something on his mind and had to have time to phrase his words. 'You must have been surprised when I issued my invitation,' he said at last. 'I trust it didn't evoke any wrong ideas — I admit I saw you once recently with a young man.'

Eric, of course. 'I was surprised, yes,' she said frankly. 'And, no, no wrong ideas. I guessed there was something you didn't wish to discuss on the ward.' It was a last-minute inspiration, and proved to be right.

'You mentioned problems before we came in to dinner. I have one of my own, and I wonder if I might take the liberty of putting it before you for your advice?'

'I'd be glad to help, if I can.'

'It's all rather too much for me. You see, a niece of my late wife is due in London from America next week on a visit. She's to be there for several days in the care of a family friend, but her parents have been in touch with me to try to find somewhere to stay outside London, somewhere which is a centre for touring — you know how keen the Americans are to see everything they think is worth seeing.

'The worrying part is that she's only fifteen, far too young to stay alone in a hotel or guest house. She'll stay here with me for a day or two, but this is rather remote, and Farnton has been mentioned. It's your home town, I know, and I wondered, do you happen to know where she could make her headquarters? A private house, preferably, where someone could keep a friendly eye on her?'

Patty thought only for a moment. 'I believe she could stay with us — with my mother and father and brother, that is. I won't be home on overnight leave for another three weeks, and we can put up a spare bed in my room if she's still there by that time. What do you think?'

'It's what you think, or, rather, what your parents think. I consider it a first-rate offer.'

'I'll phone home tomorrow as soon as I go off duty. Unless — may I phone from here?'

'Please do. I have to have a word with Mrs MacTaggart. Excuse me.' He indicated the phone and left the room.

'Is anything wrong, darling?' was Mrs

Henden's immediate reaction to hearing her daughter's voice.

Patty explained, and her mother unhesitatingly replied, 'Of course she may come here. It'll be lovely to have some feminine company. I'll get your room ready, and you can let me know when to expect her. Keep well, dear. See you soon, I hope.'

Mr Simpson must have heard the receiver being replaced. He came in almost at once, his face questioning.

'Problem solved. Mum is about to prepare the room and is waiting to hear when the young lady is to arrive.'

'I'm extremely grateful to you, Sis — er — Patty. You've taken a load off my mind. How kind and generous of your family to help us. You will, of course, find out from your mother what the — er — charge is, and tell me. I shall pay, naturally.'

'Mum would have a fit if it were put on a commercial basis,' Patty said instantly. 'She loves company and jumped at the opportunity of having another female in the house, so please don't mention that subject again!'

He smiled, a warm, light-hearted smile, giving her a glimpse of the young man whose wife, dying so prematurely, had taken his youth with her, leaving behind a sadly diminished human being.

Patty looked at her watch and jumped to her feet. 'I should get back, Mr Simpson, and you have a double journey in front of you.'

'That's not a bad thing. I find night driving very soothing and I sometimes go out for an hour in the car before I go to bed. But you have to get up even earlier than I, so I shan't keep you.'

Patty asked if she might thank Mrs MacTaggart for the meal, and once more shook the little Scotswoman's hand. 'You'll be coming back again, Miss Henden, so it's not goodbye,' Patty was assured, and blushed to find Mr Simpson standing behind her.

'I shan't hold you to that,' she said demurely as she stepped into the car. 'I do realise that you are the boss in that household!'

'I sometimes wonder myself,' he sighed, but a small smile playing round his mouth gave away the truth that he and Mrs MacTaggart knew their places.

The journey back was swift, and he didn't speak until they reached the hospital gates, then thanked her again. She found Jackie washing her hair, told her briefly the purpose of the invitation to put her mind at rest, then went straight to bed. The breath of sea air had made her drowsy, and she slept dreamlessly until her alarm clock aroused her to another day.

★ ★ ★

Beyond passing on to her mother Mr Simpson's message about Charlene's date of arrival at the Hendens' home, Patty heard nothing about the visitor until she phoned her mother some days later to say she had a full day off and would be going home. Mrs Henden had another suggestion. 'I was thinking of going through to Westingham for a change of scenery, and perhaps to take in a film, if you agree?'

'But what about Charlene?'

'I'll tell you about Charlene when I see you,' her mother said. 'Let's just say that Charlene's taken care of!' With which cryptic remark Patty had to be content until she and her mother were cosily settled with steaming cups of coffee in a quiet cafe near the bus station.

'Now, give,' Patty commanded. 'I started all this, I'm entitled to hear the best — or the worst.'

'Yes, dear. Charlene . . . Patty, when you told me she was fifteen, I thought of you at fifteen. She is not at all like you at fifteen. Charlene is like a film star of twenty-one. She not only looks glamorous — tall slim, blonde, sun-tanned, blue-eyed — rather like Dane, in fact. She also has poise and sophistication! And what clothes! When I say she took the Henden home by storm, that's an understatement!

'By the way, your Mr Simpson is rather nice. I can't understand why you described him as — what was it? — an old fossil!'

Patty looked shamefaced. 'That was when he was appointed. He's become much more human since then.'

'I should think so! He thanked me profusely when he brought Charlene to the house, and seemed pathetically glad to hand her over. He didn't stay long, refused to join us for dinner, said something about his housekeeper being annoyed if he didn't get back.'

'She does rather keep him under her thumb.'

'Anyway, back to Charlene. She's a sweetie behind that somewhat daunting appearance and manner. I was daunted, at any rate. Your father and Gerry positively lapped it up! And, Patty, don't say anything to Gerry when you see him, but I suspect he's fallen for Charlene like the proverbial ton of bricks. He immediately offered to take her wherever she wanted to go, and your dad actually said he could have the car whenever he needed it — when he wasn't using it, of course. All far beyond the normal courtesy one offers to guests.

'As I said, she's sweet, and thoughtful, too: insisted on phoning her uncle to ask permission to go out with Gerry! 'Dear old Unkie worries about me,' she said. She's a mixture of child and woman. Today she's off with Gerry with an itinerary planned out, and he's cancelled his rugby on Saturday to be available if she requires an escort! Luckily for him he has a couple of weeks' holiday from his summer job.'

'I'm impressed. Doesn't sound like my he-man brother at all. He seemed to be shaping up as a male chauvinist, too, and now a pretty blonde has him twisted round her finger!'

'To change the subject, Patty, I'm impressed with you, dear. I admit I indulged in a little worrying after you told me about Dane, but it looks as if you're being very sensible about him.'

A comment which, fortunately, needed no answer . . .

Mr Simpson seemed a little uneasy when he enquired after his niece at the ritual coffee-break on Ward Eight, and particularly concerned that she wasn't proving a burden on the family. 'She's — er — rather mature for her age,' he said one morning, and appeared to be awaiting reassurance from Patty, but she could only repeat her mother's words.

'Mum says she's sweet and thoughtful. I haven't met her myself yet, but I know that young girls today tend to act older than their age; I expect they're as unsure of themselves inside as we were.'

He appeared to be unconvinced. 'The responsibility . . . ' he murmured, and continued to look troubled.

Patty managed to behave perfectly naturally towards him now, and his manner had thawed towards Jackie. Patty was pleased at a further crack in his shell.

He'd visited the ward unexpectedly, late one afternoon. Patty had Jane Anston, the physiotherapist, in the dutyroom to hear a report of the progress in some of the ward's post-operative cases, and was listening to Jane's description of new techniques, some that she'd read about, some she'd devised on her own initiative. When he knocked and entered the room, the two looked up in surprise before jumping to their feet.

'Sorry, sir,' Patty said automatically. 'I didn't expect you. Do you wish to see one of the men?'

'I apologise for disturbing you, Sister, but yes. Peters, I think it is.'

'This morning's abdomen. I have Nurse Henry specialling him.' She led the way to the first bed in the ward, temporarily curtained off.

'If you have a moment to spare, sir, come and hear what Jane Anston's been doing,' Patty suggested impulsively as he hesitated outside the dutyroom after looking at his patient. 'She's been explaining a new routine that she's been using in orthopaedics with good results.'

He glanced at his watch. 'I can spare a few minutes, yes.'

Patty left them together and busied herself in the linen cupboard, watching for him to leave. He stayed for twenty minutes.

'Goodness, was that Mr Simpson?' Jane gasped when Patty went back to her. 'Would you believe it, that's the first time I've heard him speak more than a sentence, either ordering a treatment or changing one. He was interested — almost enthusiastic! Not his usual self at all. One could almost see him as a person, a caring person, instead of an automaton.'

'He's shy of women,' Patty told her, and added what she knew about the surgeon.

'Ah, now I understand.' Jane nodded. 'I thought it was a personal antipathy towards me.'

Jane was universally liked, by both

staff and patients. Unfailingly cheerful, she worked extremely hard and conscientiously. Patients soon got to know that her slight build and shy manner hid reserves of physical and mental strength.

It was only seniors such as Patty and Jackie, who had been years at the hospital, who knew that Jane had come back to pick up her career after her husband had walked out on her, leaving her with a small son whom she'd struggled to bring up on her own. Paul was now nine years old, an outgoing youngster with the makings of his mother's independent spirit, and Jane had confided to Patty that she'd never regretted not giving in and accepting one or other of the marriage proposals that had come her way over the years.

Some women are perfectly happy without men, Patty reflected, as Jane made for the ward doors, and, ultimately, home. She herself could never settle for a solitary life. But it would have to be the right man. And

Eric — who had called off with an unconvincing excuse what he didn't know was to be their last date — was not the one. Dane, on the other hand . . . she'd wait. Perhaps he would, indeed, come to see her again before he went back to his American home. Perhaps he'd find someone else before then . . . She put her mind to winding up the day routine before the night staff took over.

A couple of days before her next week-end leave, one of the sourer fruits of the grapevine was delivered to her door. One of her least favourite colleagues, who was rumoured to run one of the children's wards with the ruthlessness of the commanding officer of a military garrison, had something confidential to tell her, and in her usual way, prefaced her report with the disclaimer, 'I, personally, don't believe there's anything in it, Henden, but I thought you ought to know . . . '

Eric — 'that guy you're so thick with' — had been seen in a restaurant in

Farnton with a Sister from the Farnton Cottage Hospital. 'It just so happens I have a friend there who told me he's often hanging about the wards, with the excuse that one or other of his patients is hospitalised there. I know it's no business of mine, Henden, but I didn't like to think he was two-timing you.'

Patty was thankful she was able to smile with the utmost sincerity. 'Thanks for telling me. I'd do the same for you. Eric and I actually have an open-ended arrangement; it's a very casual thing so I'm not too bothered.'

The rumour was very likely true, she mused, when the woman had gone, looking disappointed. If so, it would be kind of me to break it off with him right now and save him the trouble. She went to the phone.

'This week-end, Patty?' His voice was doubtful when she told him she'd be home on Friday night, and she knew her instinct was right. 'I — er — I'm awfully sorry, I'm going to a medical convention — got a locum booked and

97

everything laid on.' His social calendar was obviously filled up.

'That's OK, Eric, I'll be pretty busy myself. I'll get in touch sometime.'

The relief in his hearty, 'Fine, Patty, do that,' was almost tangible. He understood. It was all over, and so painlessly, too. Patty was euphoric as she hurried for the bus on the Friday evening, feeling that all life was before her.

4

'Hi, Patty!' Gerry was busy with the lawnmower in the front garden when she arrived home. 'This is Charlie — Charlie, Patty.'

Patty hadn't noticed the girl kneeling at the border weeding industriously.

'Hello Charlie, Gerry — my goodness, you're working hard!'

'Hm. Charlie has this effect on people,' her brother grumbled, but his glance at the girl was affectionate.

Charlene stood up gracefully, pulled off a glove and held out her hand. 'Nice to meet you,' she said in an accent that brought Dane forcibly to Patty's mind.

Patty smiled at the girl-woman her mother had so accurately described. 'Lovely to see you both,' she said warmly, taking the small hand. 'Please excuse me, I'm off to change out of

99

uniform — one of the best parts about being home.'

'We'll be in shortly,' Gerry said. 'That's it, Charlie, we've done enough for one day.'

Mr and Mrs Henden were in the lounge sipping sherries. 'Hello, darling,' her mother said. 'Do help yourself. I'm just snatching a moment before I put the finishing touches to dinner. What do you think of Charlie? I saw you speaking to her out there.'

'Yes, what's your opinion?' her father put in. 'We think she's a little gem.'

'She's gorgeous, just as you said, Mum.' Patty put down her week-end case and poured herself a drink. 'And Gerry seems to be bowled over.'

'It was her idea to do some gardening,' said Mr Henden. 'Said she wants to repay us for our hospitality, some nonsense like that. And Gerry's like putty in her hands. Can you remember when he last cut the grass? It was in his schooldays, and I had to pay him to do it. Couldn't afford his rates these days!'

'And she insists on doing the washing-up,' his wife added. 'Calls it 'neat' to wash the dishes in a bowl and dry them with a cloth — seems everyone over there has a dishwasher!'

'She certainly seems to be a nice kid,' Patty agreed, glad the visitor was proving so popular. 'I shall report back to Mr Simpson that all is well.' She finished her drink and collected the empty glasses. 'I'll shower and change, then I'll be down to help you.'

'No need, dear.' Charlene had come into the room. 'Here's my right-hand man. You're to be guest of honour — for tonight, anyway! That's what Charlie and I have decided, isn't that right, Charlie?'

The girl grinned, showing dazzling teeth. 'Perfectly right, Mrs H. Your mom's been teaching me to bake, too,' she told Patty.

'Oh, indeed? And what happened to the busy sightseer?'

The girl looked abashed. 'Guess I got

tired of looking at old churches and things. It's much more fun going around with Gerry and his rugby guys.' She and Gerry exchanged a conspiratorial smile.

'Come with us tonight, Sis, there's a dance at the clubhouse,' Gerry urged.

'Yes, do come,' Charlie added.

'Thanks, but I don't think my feet are up to it!' Patty grimaced.

'Are you going out with Eric? Wouldn't he like to take you? You could sit out most of the dances.'

Patty hesitated for a fraction of a second. 'I'm not seeing Eric any more. And don't worry, Dad, Mum, Gerry. It was my decision. And now for a shower.' She heard her father's shocked voice as she ran lightly up the stairs, and her mother's soothing one. They'd probably banked on her settling down with Eric, and now they'd start worrying about her future. Being a parent certainly had its problems.

Mrs Henden must have briefed them: no one mentioned Eric during the meal, and even when Charlene and Gerry had left for the rugby club, her parents avoided the subject.

'Any plans for tomorrow or Sunday?' Mrs Henden wanted to know.

'You could come to golf with me,' her father suggested, before Patty could reply. The invitation, she knew, was an honour, designed to console her for the loss of Eric; he detested playing with women golfers, claiming that they slowed up the game.

'Haven't thought of anything,' Patty said. 'It's nice waiting until the last minute, then taking off. Thanks, Dad, but my golf must be completely haywire by this time. I couldn't face driving off in front of the Saturday crowds!'

In the event, she and her mother spent the morning in town, and went to a film which Mrs Henden wanted to see but which her husband condemned as 'rubbish; only fit for women'. Patty had a lazy Sunday. Her mood was still cheerful, and her mother, remembering her daughter's previous comments, agreed with her that she'd done the right thing in finishing with Eric, forbearing to add her customary, 'Someone else will turn up.'

* * *

When Mr Simpson took his seat in her dutyroom on Monday, Patty was able to give a glowing account of his niece's behaviour. What pleased him even more was the tin of chocolate chip cookies her mother had baked for him. Mrs Henden had been intrigued to find that what she thought of as an original recipe was, in fact, an American favourite.

He positively beamed, took the recipe, which Mrs Henden had written down, not without difficulty, translating her somewhat haphazard quantities into a recognisable guide. 'I shall pass this on to Mrs MacTaggart,' he said, and added, 'diplomatically,' with an unmistakable twinkle in his eye.

Patty laughed, glad for his sake that

he was softening more on each visit, and might conceivably become a real person, with human susceptibilities, one day soon. Matchmaking wasn't in her line, but she felt a little responsibility for his awakening, and wondered, in passing, if she dared think ahead to that possibility.

She had cause to be thankful that her week-end had been such a restful one. The week was hard going. Besides the scheduled cases for theatre, there had been a spate of emergencies, including a perforated duodenal ulcer and three appendicectomies. By Saturday morning she was relieved that only emergencies were being dealt with, and hoped the week-end drivers would be careful.

She was off in the afternoon, and, although the sun was shining, chose to lie on her bed with a paperback. She heard the phone and waited, hoping someone else would answer it, but no one did, and, resignedly, she went out into the corridor.

It was her mother. 'Sorry to disturb you, Patty,' Mrs Henden said. 'I phoned the office first and they told me you were off duty and might be in the Sisters' home.'

'What's wrong, Mum?' Patty sensed the tension over the telephone lines.

'Patty, it's Gerry.' Mrs Henden gulped, and went on, 'He was injured at rugby this morning.'

'Oh, Mum.' Patty had always dreaded something like this. 'How bad is it?'

'It's his spine.' Mrs Henden abandoned any pretence of self-control and burst into tears. 'Patty, he's paralysed!'

'Mum, pull yourself together. That's often only an initial condition. It doesn't necessarily mean that it's going to be permanent. Is he in the General?'

Mrs Henden blew her nose. 'Sorry for going to pieces like this. Yes, in the intensive care unit. Dad and I went up to see him, and, Patty, it's awful there.'

'Oh, Mum, it only appears like that. He has to be monitored so that they can see if his condition changes, that's all. Of course it seems terrifying when you haven't seen anyone in there before, but it doesn't mean he isn't going to get better.'

'I know you're right, Patty. But it was such a shock. He looks so — so much smaller. So weak. Oh, damn his rugby, I begged him to give it up. I should have insisted!'

'Now, for heaven's sake don't start blaming yourself. You know sport is Gerry's life, and will be again after this. What does the doctor say?'

'He says they have to stabilise him before they decide to do anything. Does that mean they might be able to operate?'

'Haven't the faintest idea, Mum. Every case is different. I can't possibly come through tonight — I'm not off till late — but tomorrow I finish at five. I'll come then, even if it's only for half an hour. I'll go straight to the hospital. There might be some good news by then. Is he in pain?'

'He's all doped up. It's ghastly. And

poor Charlie's in hysterics. They won't allow her in to see him — which is a good thing, really, she's far too young and impressionable.'

'Are you going back to the hospital now?'

'Yes. Your dad's staying there. I came home to get Charlie organised.'

'Would you phone me later? Any time after nine thirty. Let me know what's happening. And I'll see you tomorrow night.'

Being on the professional side of medicine meant you knew so many ways of curing human ills, but, on the other hand, you'd seen things going more disastrously wrong than the the lay person could even imagine, and Patty went back on duty with a picture in her mind of her beloved strong, athletic brother reduced to a cripple. It was bad enough when it happened to a stranger; unbearable to see someone close suffer so devastating a blow.

She was vividly reminded of the helpless despair that had filled her on what was, up till then, the blackest day in the existence of the Henden family. Pain gripped her at the memory of the day her father had been made redundant, and the pity had been not only for her parents, but for Gerry.

Patty had been five years old, already absorbed in school, when Gerry was born, and for her it was love at first sight. She adored the plump little baby, and took it for granted that he was equally beloved of their father and mother. Only years later did she discover that the Hendens had lost a toddler son before Patty was born, and that Gerry was doubly welcome and cherished on that account. Her parents never let her feel she was the less important of the two.

Gerry grew up, and Patty recognised that although she had the same colouring and bone structure, Gerry was a far more striking person, his good nature matching his physical excellence, and was glad for him.

They'd been so happy, as a family, so

sure life would go on as planned. Gerry had just heard of his acceptance by the college for his course in physical education, an overriding ambition since his early teens. She, Patty, was home on a week's leave. Then, at one blow, everything was threatened — their home, her parents' peace of mind, Gerry's future.

She couldn't do anything for her father, but she could help Gerry, and she did. Money she'd been saving for a continental holiday — she already had her passport — paid for his first term, and she managed to save enough from her salary for his subsequent fees. She had never spent much on herself, and didn't see that she was making any sacrifice. She vowed she wouldn't think of getting married until Gerry was qualified; there had been no difficulty in keeping her word: she hadn't met anyone since then who interested her.

Mr Henden found another, though less well-paid position. Gerry, suddenly grown up, had at once gone out looking for a part-time job, and had worked through every spare moment since, paying for books and other course requirements himself. He was to go into his final year after the summer holidays. Now this ... was it the end of a dream? ...

Ward Eight now claimed her complete attention, and when Mr Simpson made one of his unscheduled appearances near the end of her shift, her first thought was for any post-op patients he might be anxious about. But he sat down in the dutyroom with no sign of his usual impatience to go into the ward.

'Charlene telephoned me this afternoon to tell me about your brother, and I've been on to the Farnton General where I know several of the surgical team.'

His pragmatic tone steadied her, where sympathy might have provoked tears.

'X-rays have shown a fracture of a cervical vertebra. They can't tell, however, the condition of the cord, whether it's been severed or trapped, and, as you know, we are loth to go into that area when there are complications. There is one small chance, however. A great deal of research had been going on to clear the obstacles in the way of working there, and one fellow in particular has made it his speciality. We've been acquainted for a number of years, but he's abroad at the present time and it may take a day or two to locate him.

'I'm confident he'll come over and give us the benefit of his experience — young people in the lamentable position of your brother are subjects dear to his heart. I've known him travel hundreds of miles to operate in such cases, and there are numerous people of all ages walking about today who would otherwise be facing an extremely restricted future. I shall keep you in touch with developments. You are obviously tied here at present.'

Patty drew a deep breath. There was

so much to take in that it was a moment before she replied to his last statement. 'Too late to go tonight. I'm not due for any leave and there's a shortage of Sisters at this moment owing to the holidays, but I've promised my mother I'll be there tomorrow. I'm off duty at five; that should give me time to spend an hour with Gerry before I go for the last bus.'

'I may be able to drive you through, if afternoon theatre doesn't throw up any extra work. I'd like to look at your brother's X-rays and speak to the surgeon in charge, and I have to be back to be on night call.'

'That would be very kind, sir.'

'Selfish, really. I should have seen my niece before now, and I can call on her at the same time. The car would cut your journey time by half and give you longer with your brother and family. How soon after five could you be ready?'

'Ten minutes, sir. Thanks so much. You've eased my mind considerably. I was trying not to panic about Gerry, but it's not easy to be objective about one's own family.'

He nodded without speaking, and Patty regretted her choice of phrase, but knew that whatever she might add would make things worse.

'May I get a cup of tea or coffee for you, sir?'

He smiled briefly, the first sign of relaxation since he'd come in. 'No thanks, Sister. My redoubtable Mrs MacTaggart is probably already eyeing the clock and preparing my reception! Goodnight!'

★   ★   ★

Gerry lay passive, eyes closed, wired up to terminals that bleeped and flickered, a drip attached to his arm. His head was gripped by what looked like a pair of tongs, a medieval instrument of torture, and he appeared, as his mother had remarked, somehow shrunken and defenceless. His parents sat on either side of the bed, worry racking their faces. Although the ICU was a familiar scene to Patty, her heart lurched as she took in the three motionless figures, and she had to fight to keep her expression cheerful.

'He's doing well,' she told Mr and Mrs Henden, with false heartiness. 'I had a word with Sister, and she says they're all pleased with him.'

'Their pleasure is not necessarily our pleasure,' her father muttered.

'Ssh, Jack,' his wife said. 'Gerry might be able to hear us. We're confident and optimistic, Patty, no matter what your dad says. They do wonderful things for people with back injuries these days.'

Mr Henden said something under his breath about improved wheelchairs, and Patty put her arm around him.

'He's in good hands, Dad,' she said quietly. 'Mr Simpson gave me a lift here tonight so that I'd have more time to spend with Gerry, and he says they have a first-class surgical unit here, if he has to have an operation.' She wouldn't mention the possibility of a specialist being called in; he hadn't even been contacted yet, and would probably have many other commitments.

Patty had been with them for more than two hours, during which time there had been no change in Gerry, when Mr Simpson walked into the cubicle and looked carefully at him, then at the monitors.

He nodded with satisfaction towards the three anxious faces. 'We're all very hopeful of a successful outcome,' he said, and allowed a smile to soften the severity of his expression.

'Thank you, Mr Simpson,' Mrs Henden said. 'I'm sorry we had to leave Charlene in the house. My neighbour's daughter promised to keep her company.'

'She seems very much at home,' he said. 'I looked in on her a short time ago and the two girls were happily watching television. I'm most grateful to you both for your kindness to her. And now — ' he looked meaningfully at

Patty, 'I think we must make a move.'

She stood up instantly, kissed her parents, and stooped to press a kiss on her brother's forehead.

'What I didn't say in front of your parents, perhaps raising their hopes in vain,' the surgeon began, as soon as they'd cleared the city streets and emerged on to the road to Westingham, 'is that the specialist I mentioned to you has been contacted in Rome, and, as I predicted, is most interested in your brother's case. It seems likely that he can postpone some of his engagements and fit a short visit to Farnton into his schedule. They'll hear definitely tomorrow morning, and if the answer is affirmative, he could be there tomorrow night.'

'That's wonderful news!' Patty's face was alight. 'You were quite right not to mention anything to Mum or Dad; they'd be even more upset than they are if he didn't come. Oh, I do hope he does!'

Mr Simpson was operating next

morning, and paid his ward visit in the late afternoon. Patty, back from her off-duty, tried to hide her impatience as he made his round, giving each patient his usual meticulous attention. At last, back in the dutyroom, she poured his coffee and waited expectantly, trying to read in his expression what, if any, news he had about her brother.

He smiled slowly. 'Your face is like an open book, Sister.'

She coloured in confusion. 'Sorry, sir. I try not to think about Gerry, but everything I do in the ward reminds me of him.'

'Perfectly natural. So, to put your mind at temporary rest: the telephone lines have been busy between Farnton and Rome, and I'm pleased to be able to say that our man is due to arrive in London very shortly, and will hire a car and drive to Farnton. That's only the first step, as you know, but an extremely encouraging one. He'll probably study the tests and X-rays and confer with the surgical staff tonight, and if he decides to operate himself, may well do so tomorrow.'

'Oh,' breathed Patty, clasping her hands tightly and wondering how she could contrive to be at the hospital. The surgeon finished his coffee.

'I'm on call till eight a.m. tomorrow and will stay at the doctors' residence again tonight, so if you care to contact me at, say, ten p.m. I should have an up-to-date bulletin on your brother. If an operation is scheduled, I intend to be present — it's a golden opportunity to see a top man in cervical spinal surgery in action, and it so happens I have the day off.

'And you? Can you arrange some compassionate leave? Surely Miss Brendrith would look kindly on such a request at a time like this? If so, I should be pleased to take you through to Farnton again.'

'Oh, thanks, sir.' Patty hastily blinked back tears. 'If an op's on the cards for tomorrow I'll go up to the CNO first thing and see what can be done, and then call you, if I may?'

The Chief Nursing Officer was unexpectedly understanding. 'I think, with a little juggling, Sister Henden, I can manage without you for today and tomorrow. By that time we should have some of our holiday-makers back and you can let me know what the position is. You should be able to see your brother over his operation and be assured that he's past the critical stage. I hope all goes well with him.'

Patty thanked her, ashamed of the way she'd spoken about this apparently unbending, professionally-orientated woman. She joined Mr Simpson in his car an hour later, after handing over her responsibilities to Nurse Barry, who had been allocated another senior staff nurse to help her, and prepared to face the traumas that lay ahead.

The waiting-room at the Farnton General was as cheerful as could be expected: bowls of flowers, a drinks vending machine, piles of magazines, comfortable seats, and an outlook over well-tended grounds. Most of the amenities, of course, were lost on the waiting family, who were gripped by tension and foreboding.

Patty, who had so often comforted relatives of her own patients, was no less afflicted, finding herself getting up to walk to the windows, sitting down, trying to concentrate on a periodical, and, in general suffering quite as much, if not more than her father and mother.

The theatre scene kept intruding on her mind: the green-robed masked surgical team, the still figure under the lamps, the anaesthetist at the head of the table. She felt the heat, smelled the smells, heard the sounds of used instruments clinking into steel dishes, of quiet commands, of hissing oxygen and gas cylinders, of monitors printing out charts of Gerry's very life.

A young nurse looked in every so often to tell them all was going well, and on one occasion suggested they all went along to the visitors' cafeteria for a meal, promising she'd keep them in touch with any developments. Food, however, was the last thing they could face.

Conversation had long since dried up, and Patty had stopped looking at her watch, when the door opened and Mr Simpson came in, almost completely disguised in theatre greens, his mask hanging under his chin. They stared up at him, silently begging him for good news.

'The operation's over and Gerry's come through it very satisfactorily,' he said, sitting down wearily. 'The trapped cord's been released and it only remains for the fracture to knit up, which should be routine. We won't know, however, until he comes round, if movement has been restored, and even then there may be some hidden damage, but, taking into account his youth, this should heal in due course. Some patience is required, but the prognosis is good.'

Tears were running down Mrs Henden's face. 'Thank God,' she said, 'and thanks to the surgeons. I suppose we couldn't see them to thank them personally?'

'Mum, no. They'll be dead beat, and probably have a huge list to get through today,' Patty said urgently.

Mr Simpson held up a hand to stop her. 'I'll see what I can do. Wait here.'

Mrs Henden was wiping her eyes, and her husband was staring unseeingly out of the window when Mr Simpson came back with a small chubby man in tow, hair ruffled, white coat flying open, face beaming. 'This is Mr Scott,' he told the Hendens. 'Chief general surgeon of the hospital.'

They were all on their feet now, and Mr and Mrs Henden broke into a stumbling flurry of thanks, which the little man waved away with a cheerful smile. 'Nonsense. No thanks to me. I was simply the assistant at this operation. Here's the man to thank, the man who's travelled thousands of miles to share the skill of his magic fingers — '

Patty followed his gesture towards

the door, and, in stunned disbelief, saw the tall tanned figure make his entry. Mr Simpson was performing an introduction, but it was Mrs Henden who found her voice first. 'Dane!' she cried out, and threw her arms around him. He smiled, gently disengaged himself from her embrace, and looked at Patty.

'I'm glad I was able to help,' he said, speaking as though she were the only person in the room.

The shock was too great. This time she couldn't keep control, and tears spilled over. He stepped towards her, and, regardless of the audience, enveloped her in his arms.

She didn't hear that the silence was broken simultaneously by Mr Henden's astonished 'What's going on?' and Mr Simpson's embarrassed cough. Her cheek was pressed against Dane's chest, and she listened to the hammering of his heart, marvelling that they shared the same overwhelming emotion. This was the man she loved, she could never doubt it, or wonder if her love was returned.

How could she have failed to connect his year abroad with Mr Simpson's description of the visiting surgeon? How was it that Mr Simpson knew him well enough to find him? There were so many questions to be answered, and so little time.

'I knew Lou, Ronnie Simpson's wife, in college,' Dane told them later. He had come back to the Hendens' home at Mrs Henden's invitation. 'She met Ronnie when she was in the UK on vacation and they visited with each other back and forth across the Atlantic until they married. I'd met him frequently, in London and in LA, and kept in touch after Lou died. Ronnie was inconsolable, clammed up tight, and is still a bit prickly.

'Neither of us is good at writing letters, but I let him know when this idea of mine came up, to take a year off to do a round of teaching hospitals in Europe. We expected to meet, of course, but we'd left the date open. I didn't dream it would be so soon, and in such circumstances, but I'm glad I was able to help someone I know — ' his smile was for Patty.

'When did you know it was Gerry?' Mrs Henden queried.

'Not until I saw the results of his tests last night. Then I remembered Patty telling me about him, and that he was mad keen on rugby; my antennae signalled a warning at that point, but what could I do? Baseball is my constant enemy in the States.' He sighed. 'Can't stop the kids flinging themselves around, but it sure makes work for us!'

'But how do you know Patty?' Mr Henden was clearly bewildered by the turn of events, and his wife quickly hushed him up, explaining that she'd tell him later.

Charlene, eyes huge in her lovely face, drank in the conversation, for once stuck for words, her poise having deserted her, leaving a troubled teenager. 'Have you saved Gerry's life?' she ventured at last, addressing Dane.

'Ah, a fellow countryman!' Dane beamed at her.

'Charlene's Mr Simpson's niece,' Mrs Henden told him. 'She's staying with us for a holiday.' The girl was still gazing up at him, entreaty in her eyes.

'I've done my very best,' he said to her. 'It's all up to nature now. Gerry's in superb physical condition, and that has to have a bearing on the healing process. So you can take that mournful look off your face and let him see a smile when you visit with him.'

'They won't let me in yet.'

'Much too soon,' Dane nodded. 'Give him a few days and he'll be the guy you know. He wouldn't like you to see him as he is just now . . . Ronnie's niece, are you? Not Miriam's daughter?'

The girl nodded eagerly. 'You know her?'

'Sure do. She was the prettiest of the three girls, and I guess you take after her.'

That made everything all right. Charlene blushed prettily, murmured a soft, 'Thanks,' and looked more cheerful.

The family had taken heart at Dane's words, and Mrs Henden suggested tea. 'Stay if you can, Dane — er — Doctor Culver,' she said hospitably, 'or is it Mr Culver?'

'Dane, please. We're friends, aren't we? Another hour, perhaps, then I must get back to my patient. I've left this telephone number, but I don't expect to hear anything until Gerry comes round.' He turned to Patty, who was sitting quietly, her eyes on his every move. 'Come into the garden, Patty.'

Mr Henden had placed a rustic seat strategically behind a long-established rhododendron bush, and there, hidden from the house, Dane took her into his arms hungrily. She closed her eyes and gave herself up to his kiss, all thought suspended.

'My dear, dear girl.' He put her away from him and studied her face. 'I've thought of nothing and no one else since I left you. You've been my Madonna, watching over me. I've had to restrain myself over and over again from coming back and abandoning the rest of the tour. I've cursed myself for planning a whole year of travel — and yet, would we have met otherwise?

'Patty, it's a lot to ask, but, please, please — I have to complete this schedule, I've given my word to so many people, and what I have to tell them is so important, I've spent years on it. Oh, I know I'm not making sense, but, Patty, please tell me I may come back to you — for good?'

For answer, she stood on tiptoe to reach his lips, and he strained her to him, more roughly this time. The urgency of his desire lit a fire within her, and the garden, the sunshine, and all sense of time were obliterated as her senses focused on one compelling need.

When he pulled her down beside him on the garden seat, she was breathless. 'I can't risk losing you, Patty. We're going to be married — right?' She nodded, eyes shining. 'How can I make you a proper fiancée without a ring, and there's no time to buy one?'

She laughed tremulously. 'I'll wait for you, Dane, ring or no ring.'

'You'll come back with me to LA? A foreign country? Leave your family and friends?'

'They'll come to visit us. I'll have you.'

'My dearest.' He kissed her again, long and ardently. 'There's David — will you mind if he visits with us?'

'I'll love having him.'

'And — and — kids of our own?'

'Them too!' Them most of all, she said silently.

'Tea's ready!' Mrs Henden sang out, and the interlude was over.

'I'm staying at the hospital tonight, tomorrow and the next day if necessary, to see the outcome of the operation. I'll see you there, OK? By the way, where do you nurse?'

'Ronnie's hospital, in Westingham.'

'Really? I have a lecture date there towards the end of my year. He made me promise not to miss it out. But I'll be over here before then.'

She was with her brother next day, her parents persuaded to go for lunch, when he came into the unit, professional in stiff white coat, accompanied by the chief surgeon. Out of habit, she stood up respectfully, and he waved her down again.

He bent to examine Gerry, who had come round and had been dozing on and off. Now Dane touched his cheek. 'Hi, Gerry, let's have a word out of you.'

The boy's eyes flickered open and he looked hazily into Dane's face. 'Who are you?' His speech was slurred with sleep.

'I'm the guy who's tried to get you out of the mess you got yourself into, and this here is the chief surgeon, Mr Scott. Are you going to show us what you can do with your toes? Come along, let's see a wiggle.' He'd turned back the bottom of the sheet and Patty's eyes followed theirs, her mind willing a movement. There was the slightest tremor.

'Good work, Gerry, a little more, now! Do it for Patty!'

Gerry's eyes turned to her and he smiled faintly. 'It's not easy, you know!' He produced a slight but definite twitch.

'Good lad.' Dane patted his hand. 'You're on the mend. Take it slowly, and you'll do.'

To the surgeon, he said, 'I'm going for lunch shortly, then I'll see you in your office, if that's suitable?' The little man agreed and walked away.

Gerry was watching them sleepily.

'This is Dane,' Patty said. 'Mr Culver. He did the op you had yesterday and I'm going to marry him.'

'Gosh,' he got out. 'Fast work. Do the parents know?'

'Not yet. I'll break the news later. Go back to sleep now, they'll be back from lunch soon. I'll wait here until they come.' His eyes closed.

Dane looked out at the nurses' station then came back and kissed Patty quickly and thoroughly. 'I don't believe I can go on for the rest of my year without you. I'll phone wherever I am, and write a letter or two, so you can keep track of me. You have to take me on trust, Patty. I love you.'

'I trust you. And I love you, too.'

When her parents came back, Patty and Dane found a small cafe near the hospital where they sat holding hands and toying with sandwiches and coffee. The reaction after the worry about Gerry, and the magical arrival of Dane had gone to Patty's head, and she felt she'd never been so happy.

Dane, set on giving her his life-story, looked boyishly enthusiastic as he told her about his family, his schooling and his years of study, but when he came to his interest in spinal surgery, the boy changed into a compassionate man.

'It happened to a guy in the university baseball team. I only knew

133

him by sight, but he was a mighty player, powerful and broad-shouldered. There was a mid-pitch collision, and Josh was still lying there when the other player got to his feet. I heard the coach yell, 'Don't move him!' and he was left as he was until the paramedics came for him. They tried some last-ditch surgery but that didn't help. He never walked again.

'God.' He shook his head. 'Imagine spending the rest of your life in a wheelchair! I swore I'd dedicate my professional career to helping to prevent that. You must have gone through hell when you heard about Gerry?'

She nodded. 'Thank you for what you did for him.'

'Happy to have been able to get here. He should mend naturally, now, and I'll be off back to Italy tomorrow if all goes well between now and then. Scott's more than competent enough to take it from there . . . Patty, I want to speak to you and to hug you at least once a day. I've been aching to touch you. I'd like us to be married right away, but we'd still have to be apart — my mind wouldn't be on my commitments if I knew you were waiting for me in some hotel room. So we have to be patient, and I must go. The sooner I return to my schedule the sooner the year will be completed. And then . . . '

She smiled into his eyes. 'And then . . . '

5

'Then' became more remote instead of nearer as the days went on. A subdued celebration of Patty's and Dane's unofficial engagement was overlaid with anxiety for Gerry, whose full recovery threatened to be a slow one. Dane flew back to Italy and Patty returned to the hospital. A tearful Charlene was persuaded to kiss Gerry goodbye and depart soon after.

Patty came down to earth gradually. After three attempts at reaching her by phone had proved useless, she being off-duty each time and out of the hospital, Dane had had to resort to letters. He was moving around, lecturing here and there, continually having to reorganise his schedule when cases cropped up where he was called in for consultation and often agreed to operate. It was a punishing tour and she understood when the letters became fewer.

He'd used up considerable space in one recounting a tricky operation on a young girl who had been involved in a motor-cycle accident. It seemed he'd been taken into the warm hearts of Mama and Papa, and was being overwhelmed by their hospitality.

The girl, Olivia, had tugged at Dane's heart-strings. 'She's so young,' he wrote. 'I wasn't sure she'd come through, but there was a core of strength inside her, and she's fighting bravely. She's an exquisite child, black-eyed, black-haired. And there's an elder daughter with the same colouring. I told the family right away I was engaged to a beautiful English nurse, but I think they'd like to present Donna to me as a reward for operating on their adored Olivia! It's a great compliment, of course, but no temptation, dearest, I assure you!'

The Italian family were mentioned again in his next letter, postmarked

Naples. 'Olivia is coming along nicely, and they've invited me to go with them to Sorrento for a short vacation. They have a villa there, and there's a space in my diary — a long weekend. The thought of swimming and sailing is more than I can resist — the heat here is oppressive. Patty, dear, if only you were with me in this incomparable country!'

Patty was off herself that weekend, and went home, nerves jangling. Jealousy is an occupational hazard of most doctors' fiancées and wives, she told herself, and is usually completely unfounded, but that didn't stop the pangs of almost physical pain that shot through her when she thought of Dane and Donna in the glorious Italian sunshine, swimming together, sunbathing together, 'together' being the disturbing word in the imaginary scenes.

She tried to be rational about her feelings, but already the memory of Dane's hypnotic effect on her was fading, and as she sat in the kitchen on the Saturday morning after breakfast and listened to her mother making excited plans for a wedding, she felt depressed that she no longer shared Mrs Henden's dreams.

'Mum, don't say any more about weddings,' she pleaded, and was at once contrite when she saw her mother's troubled expression. 'We haven't broken up, but — well — a year is a long time. Anything can happen.' I haven't even his ring, she said to herself. Would it make any difference, though, if I had? Engagements are often broken.

'You still hear from him?'

'Oh yes. He writes when he can. He's been extremely busy and this weekend he's having a break in Sorrento.'

'How lovely! I'm sure he deserves it.'

'With an Italian family. In their villa. He operated on their young daughter. They have another daughter. Dane says she's beautiful ... 'Exquisite' is the word he used.'

Mrs Henden put away the breakfast

dishes she'd been drying, and sat down opposite her daughter. 'Darling, I do believe you're just the least bit jealous!'

'True,' Patty admitted gloomily. 'And not without reason. Sun and sea and Donna and Dane. Seems a potent combination.'

'Only if you put the parts together the wrong way. Dane told you about Sorrento and about Donna, didn't he? Now, if he had any intentions towards the girl, would he have mentioned her?'

'He may not have realised how he'd feel when they were — together.'

'And you do? Patty, that sounds like a penny novelette! Dane's seen hundreds of pretty girls — California's full of them — yet he chose you. Are you going to be like this when you're married — suspecting him of falling in love with every female nurse and patient? If so, that's the sure way to lose him.'

Patty didn't answer. Lately she'd forgotten at times what Dane looked like, and had no photographs to refresh her memory with, but now she had a vivid picture of him in her mind: devastatingly handsome, with the physique of an athlete. Charming. Divorced.

His wife had divorced him. Why? He'd be unlikely to tell the truth to her or anyone else. Being a doctor, or a nurse, gave no immunity to the appeal of the opposite sex; increased it, sometimes. And hadn't Dane picked her, Patty, up, in the first instance? Thinking she was, at the most, eighteen? Perhaps he had a penchant for young girls? Did she know him at all? What kind of a life would she live with him, in an unknown country? Her eyes, raised to her mother, were wretched with despair.

The ring of the telephone forestalled Mrs Henden's next words. 'Er — yes, she is,' she answered a query haltingly, looking at Patty. 'Hang on, I'll see if she's around.' To Patty she said, 'It's Eric, do you want to speak to him?'

Patty made an instant decision. 'It's

me, Eric,' she said, taking the receiver from her mother's hand. 'No, I've made no plans . . . All right, seven o'clock.' She looked challengingly at her mother. 'I'm going out with him, to a film, and supper afterwards. If Dane can do it, so can I, and don't make any comment, Mum, I'm quite old enough to know what I'm doing.'

'That's fine, Patty. I wasn't going to say anything. Now, tell me what you'd like to do this morning.'

After lunch, Patty and her parents went to visit Gerry. He was in a ward now, visiting hours strictly controlled. He looked more like the old Gerry, although he was still lying on his back, his head held in hyper-extension. He was patently glad to see them.

'Got a letter from Charlie today,' he said triumphantly. 'She hasn't forgotten me yet.'

'How could anyone forget you?' Patty teased. 'Once seen, and all that. How's your physiotherapy going?'

'Great. I've got the dishiest girl — a

red-head with huge violet eyes. Looks fragile, but she's got muscles of steel.'

'Ah. Do I detect a wandering eye?' his sister observed.

'Just being sociable,' he said airily. 'She'd have a lousy job if no one spoke to her, wouldn't she?' He was improving rapidly, a little more movement coming back each day.

'How's the boy-friend?' he asked Patty.

'He's got very little time to call his own.' She was aware of her mother's steady regard. 'Your complaint is an extremely common one, unfortunately.'

'Give me his latest address before you go, Patty,' her father said. 'I must write to him from all of us to thank him for what he did for Gerry.' Mrs Henden nodded in agreement.

'Tell him I was asking for him,' Gerry added. 'Imagine, he's going to be my brother-in-law! Good old Patty! We never thought she'd marry a celebrity. And what a bonus having a sister living in California! Holidays galore! And I've always wanted the chance to play an American team at baseball!'

His visitors shuddered in horrified accord. 'For heaven's sake, boy!' Mr Henden's voice rose and the people at nearby beds looked over. 'Aren't you in enough trouble? Dane told me nearly all his work in the US is on baseball casualties!'

'Only kidding, Dad,' Gerry apologised, and watched them relax. 'I'm very grateful to Dane and I assure you I shan't undo his good work. 'Caution' will be my middle name from now on. The rugby chaps are talking about making me their non-playing captain, so that'll keep me on the sidelines.'

The prognosis for her brother was good, and Patty joined Eric later in a mood of reckless abandon, leaving her mother to explain away the date to her father any way she chose. In the cinema, Eric took her hand, and, after only a slight hesitation, she allowed it to remain in his. He'd booked a table at one of the better restaurants, and she'd put all feelings of guilt to the back of her mind by the time they were consulting the menu.

Eric had been unusually attentive. Guilty conscience? she wondered, as he waved the waiter aside and drew out the chair for her, arranging her jacket on the back of it. He'd decided to give me up, that's for sure, but he must have been thrown over himself! She smiled to him across the table and his returning look was warm.

As they waited for the main course, her glance roved idly round the room and stopped at a corner table, her heart jolting in shock. Ronald Simpson was sitting facing her, and couldn't miss seeing her! What appalling luck! The only person outside the family who knew both her and Dane. He must know about their unofficial engagement; the two men kept in contact.

Her eyes were fixed on him in helpless compulsion when he looked over and spotted her. He nodded gravely in recognition and went on talking to his male companion. Someone from the Farnton General, no doubt. She felt herself grow cold, then hot, and thought wildly of what she could say to Mr Simpson on his next ward visit to let him know that Eric was only a friend.

'He's undertaken the year's itinerary entirely at his own expense,' the surgeon had told her soon after Dane had gone back to Italy. She'd listened eagerly, avid to hear something about Dane that she didn't already know. 'He's been generous with his services for the last few years, lecturing during his vacations, and flying here, there and everywhere when he was called on . . . You'll forgive my mentioning it, Sister, but — er — you and he — you are old friends, too?'

She'd blushed. 'Not at all. I met Dane — Mr Culver — quite by chance just before he left for Europe.' It wasn't easy talking about personal matters to the surgeon, who, although he'd mellowed considerably, still evoked in her instincts of respect to someone on a higher level in hospital than herself.

He nodded ambiguously and changed the subject. Seeing him now in the restaurant was the worst thing that could happen, and Patty was effectively subdued, to the extent that even Eric, essentially self-obsessed, felt the coolness in the atmosphere between them.

'Have I said something wrong?' he demanded.

'No, of course not,' she said hastily. 'It's just that — I'm rather tired.'

He frowned. 'You're always tired,' he said, with a touch of impatience. 'If only you'd be sensible and marry me, you'd have time for everything, without wearing yourself out over strangers. What about it, Patty? We've both sown our wild oats — ' Patty looked at him in indignation; how dared he compare her to himself? ' — Don't look at me like that, I'm quite sure you've had the odd affair since you've been nursing, all nurses do, and I shan't ask you about any of them. We'll both start off with clean slates, how about that?'

She'd been incredibly stupid in accepting this invitation, Patty saw, but it must be the last, whether or not Dane ever heard about it.

'Eric,' she said carefully, concentrating on making her point as clearly as possible; she'd been far too vague the last time. 'I'm sorry to turn you down again, but I don't love you and I won't marry you. Please don't be hurt. Thank you for tonight, I've enjoyed it, but I'd rather not go out with you again and let you hope that I might change my mind.'

There, it was said, clumsily but conclusively. His face reddened in annoyance. 'Well, you're the loser,' he said roughly.

'Yes, I may well be' she agreed appeasingly, 'but I'm sure you'll find someone who's more — more — '

More what? She'd like to have said 'slavish' or, perhaps, 'gullible', decided he wouldn't appreciate their significance, and finished ' — adaptable than I am.'

They finished the meal in an uncomfortable silence, she once more assailed by a deep yearning for Dane, he, no doubt, deciding which Farnton nurse he'd date the following week. They didn't prolong the evening.

At home there was a message from her friend Sheila, who asked her to return the call before she went back to the hospital. Patty rang her in the morning.

'Patty, I'm glad I caught you on a week-end off. There's a place on the next district nursing course — a girl I know has cancelled — and I immediately thought of you. You said you were thinking about your future the last time we met, remember? Why not come over to lunch today and we can discuss it; I'll fill you in with any details you want to know.'

★   ★   ★

Patty found her friend busy and happy, and sat down to lunch with Sheila's accountant husband Tim, and their toddler Ben. 'And, guess what, I'm pregnant again!' Sheila had whispered joyfully while Patty was still on the doorstep.

The house was comfortably untidy, Ben's toys lying around, Tim's papers stacked on a side table, Sheila's magazines and knitting on a chair. 'We'll get lunch over then Tim's going to take Ben out for a walk and give us a bit of peace,' Sheila explained.

As soon as Tim and Ben had departed, with a tricycle and a couple of soft toys in tow, the two girls sat down with another cup of coffee, and Sheila launched into a description of the intensive training intended to fit senior nurses into the demands of the district.

Patty found her attention wandering. She felt at home in the rather shabby armchair in the near-chaos of a family house. Sheila, in the early stages of her pregnancy, was radiant; there was no doubt that she'd found her niche in life. Patty had lost herself in a dream of carrying Dane's baby when Sheila stopped talking.

'You're miles away, Patty,' she reproved her friend. 'What or whom are you dreaming about?'

'Sorry. A momentary lapse. Go on, it's fascinating.'

'I don't think so. From the glassy look in your eye you're in love with someone and thinking of all that goes with it!'

Patty laughed. 'You're far too perceptive. Well, yes, you're partly right. I've met a lovely man, and I hope we may marry some day.'

'Some day! Why the delay? Get him and tie him down, that's my motto.'

Patty chuckled, remembering how assiduous Tim was in tying a somewhat flirtatious younger Sheila down.

'Heavens, you make him sound like a cross between a steer and a fish. As if I've caught him and have to hang on.'

'Well, it's true, you have to do a bit of fighting. There's so much competition about. Come on, tell me the story; I scent a small dilemma.'

Patty gave her an outline, and as she spoke, her fears about the Sorrento week-end seemed weak and groundless.

'Oh, dear, this sounds like a letter to the problem page! Why on earth don't you simply go over and see what he's up to? Even if you manage only a few hours with him? I agree that Donna's there and you're here, and anything could happen, but of course it won't, as you well know, and you were idiotic to play around with Eric when you'd given a promise to Dane. Still, no doubt you've learned your lesson.'

'Go over to Italy? I never thought of that. But how?'

'Patty, don't be such a wimp. You have your passport from that Spanish holiday you were planning, you'll be due another week-end off soon, and you have, presumably, heard of planes? It'll cost you a bit, but it'll be worth it to put your mind at rest. If I were Dane I'd have suggested your going out there and getting married without waiting for the year to be up, but from what you tell me he hasn't even thought of that. He's so absorbed in his patients that his fiancée, and, ultimately, his wife, will come a poor second. You are prepared for that possibility, I take it?'

Patty hung her head. 'I thought I was. Never thought I'd be jealous. Jealousy hurts, did you know?'

'So I've heard. Never suffered from it myself. You'll have to take yourself in hand if you decide to marry a doctor — you've seen enough in hospital, surely, to know what goes on, what temptations lurk? And that's a perfectly valid reason for doing your district training before you get married. That way, while he's busy with his patients, you'll be busy with yours, with no time to think too deeply. Well?'

'One snag. He's American. Don't suppose they have the same nursing schemes there, and certainly not on a national health service basis.'

'Ah, American! Wonder why you didn't mention that, eh? Worrying about his status back home, I guess!'

'He's divorced. And has a little boy — his ex has custody.'

'More complications.' Sheila sighed. 'Nothing's ever straightforward, is it? There was Eric laying everything out on a plate, but that wasn't satisfactory either. So, this one's American. Well, Sheila's advice still stands: get yourself out to Italy and clear things up — for the moment, anyway. Give yourself time to find out more about his background before you marry the guy, if that bugs you, and, in the meantime, start your district training.'

'So that I'll have something to fall back on if . . . ?' Patty suddenly felt desolate.

'You have to face up to that possibility,' her friend counselled. 'It may never happen, but then again that old saying, 'Marry in haste — ' too often comes true. Now, have I thoroughly depressed you?'

Patty's face cleared. 'No. You've made me see things more clearly. I love him, Sheila. I've never wanted anyone before the way I want him. But it's hard to go on loving when you're so far apart. And, no, I don't think I'll apply for that vacancy. Maybe next year . . .'

She went back on duty, fired by Sheila's practical suggestion to visit Dane. When she knew her next week-end off, she'd check his schedule. She'd find the money somehow — Gerry's next term was covered; it meant just a few more economies. It would be worth it to see Dane. She would book the flight with a local travel agent. No point in telling Dane she was going over; her leave could be cancelled up to the last minute. She'd phone her mother the evening before she left. She'd brought her passport and a couple of light dresses from home and would go straight to the airport . . .

Staff Nurse Barry was good. Patty could find no fault with the ward, the ante-rooms or the case histories. Barry would be promoted to Sister soon, there was no doubt about that, and although Patty would be sorry to lose her, she knew the promotion would be well deserved.

They sat in the dutyroom for a few minutes as Patty caught up with the newest admissions, Saturday's discharges, and the day's theatre list. There was a full complement of staff on duty, for a change, and sounds of coming and going, snatches of conversation from patients, clatter from the kitchen and the occasional clang from the sluice combined to form a comforting background.

Barry was Welsh, red-haired and green-eyed, and her eyes seemed to sparkle more than usual.

'You're positively glowing this morning, Nurse,' Patty observed.

The girl's ivory skin turned pink. 'Got engaged yesterday, Sister! Look!' she fished inside the neck of her uniform dress and pulled out a gold chain on which was strung a diamond ring.

'Congratulations! I didn't realise things had got to such a serious stage.'

'I gave him a bit of a push, really,' Nurse Barry confessed. 'Eddie's a good chap, but a little slow. Getting married at Christmas.'

Patty raised her eyebrows. 'You'll stay on here, of course?'

The girl shook her head. 'Not me! We're both going back to Wales and I'm going to be a housewife until the babies arrive. We want a big family.'

'I was looking forward to giving you a good report when the CNO decided you were ready for promotion.'

'Being a Sister's nothing compared to being married and having your own kids,' Nurse Barry said firmly. 'And now that I've brought Eddie to the point, I'm impatient to be gone. Not that I haven't enjoyed nursing, and I've been very happy on men's surgical with you, Sister.'

'I'll miss you, Barry, but if your

mind's made up, that's it.'

Barry and Jackie, both marrying at Christmas! Nice, thought Patty, basking in her staff nurse's glow, and identifying with it, although the chasm between an agreement to marry and the actual ceremony appeared to her at that moment to be unbridgeable.

There was something of an international gathering in the ward just then. Several Pakistanis were recovering from surgery. Their female visitors made an exotic picture in their delicate, floating saris, and the children were irresistible with their huge liquid black eyes. She often longed to cuddle one of the youngsters, but felt any contact might be resented by the mothers, some of whom still seemed to lead a confined life.

'Good morning, Mr Singh, how's the leg today?' The man lay with one leg, with fractured tibia and fibula, slung up in traction, his high bed festooned with ropes and pulleys to enable him to pull himself up.

'Great, Sister,' he said cheerfully. 'Apart from missing my vindaloos, I've no complaints. And my sons think I'm having a ball — they go home and try to rig up a bed like mine with poles and ropes and goodness knows what not!'

Young Khaled was less outgoing. Patty sat down on the side of his bed and regarded him sympathetically. His appendix had flared up on the eve of an important college exam, and he'd been depressed about having to give up his part-time labouring job which, he'd told her, was essential to top up the college grant. Today, however, he looked happier.

'My uncle's giving me a part-time job in his clothing factory,' he told her, with a shy smile. 'In the office. So I won't do any damage here — ' he patted the site of his operation. 'And I'll apply to re-sit my exam. That'll give me time to do some more swotting, too!'

Mr Rashid was having his wound dressed. Patty took a mask in its envelope out of her pocket and stepped behind the curtains to watch Nurse Barry as she swabbed the dressing and the area around it and gently peeled it away. The elderly man, whose white hair contrasted with his brown skin, had been injured in an explosion at his work and several small slivers of glass were still embedded in one shoulder.

Nurse Barry used a local anaesthetic spray before she took a pair of fine forceps from the dressings trolley and began to probe for splinters; they'd come to the surface eventually.

'Does it hurt badly, Mr Rashid?' Patty asked.

'No, thank you, Sister.' He'd been born in Pakistan and had never lost his accent. 'Nurse Barry is very — very slow, very careful. She like you, Sister, she no want us to have any pain.' He smiled, but it was clear he was uncomfortable.

'Leave it for now, Nurse,' Patty said after a few minutes. 'I'll have a go this evening.'

'Thank you,' the old man said gratefully.

A young Chinese waiter from one of the city's restaurants had been burned when a pan of hot oil caught fire in the kitchen. He'd suffered a lot of pain, with only the occasional plea for relief, but he, too, was improving, and greeted Patty with a smile.

'Are you feeling a bit easier now, Mr Lee?'

'Oh, yes, very little pain now.'

'You'll soon be going home. Your treatment will be completed in outpatients.'

'Very good news, Sister. You will come to my restaurant for a chop suey? Come with your husband.'

'Thanks, Mr Lee. I'm not married, but I'll pop in with one of my colleagues, if I may. We both love Chinese food. How is your beautiful daughter?' Patty had met his wife one visiting day. She'd asked permission to bring the child into the ward, apologetic that she had no one to leave her with.

She was an adorable doll-like tot with almond eyes, creamy skin and straight, shining hair cut with a fringe.

Mr Lee's face lit up with pleasure. 'She is well, thank you, also my wife. They may visit today.'

A Scot completed the 'foreign' contingent, an accountant who'd been educated at an English public school and had a perfectly modulated voice, but who took a fiendish delight in speaking in a broad dialect to baffle the nursing staff.

'Ah'm no bad the noo, Sister,' he said in answer to her enquiry as to his well-being. 'Ah canna get thae taiblets the doc ordered doon ma gullet, though. Kin ye no do something aboot that? Ah get into a fair fankle when Ah have tae swallow them!'

'Ay, Ah'll dae something about it,' she answered impishly, then reverted to English. 'I take it you do mean the sleeping tablets are rather large to swallow?'

'Yes, Sister, I do, indeed I do.' He was

back to the suave professional man. 'They're like rocks!'

'I'll ask one of the night nurses to crush them for you,' she promised.

It was good to see them progressing. Patty had a warm feeling inside when she left the ward and went to prepare for the visit, and thought not for the first time, how satisfying it was to nurse surgical patients.

The phone rang — a renal colic was coming up from casualty, in time to catch Mr Simpson. She sent Nurse Henry to check that Mr Harrison's bed had been changed and was made up for the next arrival, the locker emptied and scrubbed, and that Mr Harrison himself, a prostatectomy, was safely in the day room waiting for his wife to collect him. Also, to see that a diagnostic trolley was set.

Mr Simpson was distant, somehow distraught. He did his visit with a frown on his face, and Patty thought he sighed when the trolley with the new patient came into the ward just as he was finishing. He examined the man with his usual thoroughness, however, read the notes that came up with him, and gave Doctor Dykes and Patty the usual instructions — medication, tests, X-rays.

Mr Davidson, a man in his forties, lay sweating quietly, recovering from a bout of excruciating pain, and Mr Simpson patted his shoulder sympathetically before he left him. 'We'll clear it all up,' he reassured him, and the man smiled weakly.

The surgeon's face seemed more drawn and gaunt than usual, Patty thought, when he slumped into her chair in the dutyroom.

'Is anything wrong, sir?'

He hesitated. 'Small problem,' he said tersely. 'Hardly worth mentioning.'

Medical personnel were notoriously chary of consulting their doctors, Patty reflected, but decided it was hardly her place to suggest that he have a word with Mr Callans. The chief general surgeon was an easy-going man who gladly left most of the theatre action to his underlings, remaining available for consultation.

It was said of him among the doctors that he was 'past it', and that they'd rather suffer than entrust themselves to old Henry. Profanity, of course, Patty and Jackie had assured themselves, fingers crossed, however, 'for you never know when Simpson and Sturgess will both be off at the same time and Henry will be free to do his worst.'

Mr Simpson finished his coffee, refused a biscuit, and took his leave. It hadn't been the time to try to explain away her appearance at the restaurant with Eric, and, in fact, the whole episode had lost its significance. She'd soon be with Dane, and nothing else would count.

During the next couple of weeks, Patty refused Jackie's offer of a loan to help pay for the journey, and booked flights to and from Naples, where Dane was due to lecture on the Friday and Saturday of the week-end she was to be off. She noticed on the map with a sinking heart how near Sorrento was, and tried not to worry about the proximity of Donna. Jackie had an Italian woman on her ward, and Patty spent an hour or two with her, jotting down a basic vocabulary, and listening to her lyrical description of that part of her native land.

'Naples!' she said, blowing a kiss in its general direction, 'Naples is of the most beautiful! You are so lucky to go there. Is a place for love!'

Ward Eight was certainly no place for anything but work, and by lunchtime on the Friday before her carefully planned jaunt abroad, Patty barely had time to snatch a sandwich for her midday snack. Jackie was sympathetic. 'Wish there was something I could do for you, but I'm short-handed right now. In fact, can't see myself getting any time off next week at all. We've had a spate of traffic accidents — and it won't surprise you to know that no women drivers were involved in any of them — my patients are the victims of a male-orientated society! Mown down by the very MCPs who devote their lives to trying to make us look fools!'

Patty laughed at her friend's indignation. 'My, my! Is this what comes of being too long on a female ward? What would you be like if you were a libber?'

'No chance of that,' Jackie retorted. 'And see that you don't turn into one! Grab that man, do you hear? Make sure the detestable Donna knows that you're promised to him, and don't let him go!'

I won't, Patty vowed to herself. She returned to the ward, confident that nothing had been overlooked in the arrangements for reaching Dane, and conscious of a flutter of excitement — more, a deepening desire — at the thought of being with him again in only a few hours' time. The fruition of her plans, however, though she couldn't foresee it, was to differ a great deal from the blueprint.

6

Footsteps down the corridor — heavy masculine steps; Mr Simpson wasn't expected, but there he stood, and Patty saw at a glance that the surgeon was unwell.

As she wasn't due to leave for Italy until the Saturday morning, she'd exchanged shifts with her staff nurse, letting Nurse Barry off at five p.m., to her delight, and taking her own off-duty in the afternoon. Now, Barry not long gone, Patty had settled down to the evening's work, and was brought abruptly to her feet as Mr Simpson stumbled in and collapsed on to a chair.

She eyed him narrowly. He was feverish, flushed, eyes over-bright, and, unprotestingly, he allowed her to place a thermometer under his tongue, and hold his wrist. Pulse and temperature both up. As she replaced the thermometer he suddenly bent over and vomited over the floor.

'Oh, God, I'm sorry, Sister.' He groaned, arms tucked round his middle. 'Appendix, I think.'

Patty lifted the phone. 'Doctor Dykes to Ward Eight, stat,' she ordered crisply. Two of the student nurses were on. She called them. 'Help me get Mr Simpson into the side room,' she instructed. Thank goodness the bed was empty. It wasn't always easy to keep one for an emergency. The surgeon tried to help himself, but was obviously in some pain. Patty sent one of the nurses for a kidney dish in anticipation of more sickness, settled him on the bed, loosened his clothing and drew the covers over him.

Doctor Dykes had wasted no time in answering Patty's call. At first uncertain about examining his chief, he soon realised that the man was in no state for formality. A quick palpation caused Mr Simpson to wince, then he pulled himself up on his side and was sick again, straining over the dish which Patty managed to position just in time.

The junior doctor's eyes met Patty's, and he nodded almost imperceptibly in reply to her questioningly arched eyebrows as Mr Simpson flopped back in exhaustion. Patty wiped the sweat from his brow.

'Appendix?' he queried.

'Yes, sir.'

'Get Callans. He'll have to operate right away.' He closed his eyes as the doctor went over to the dutyroom.

'Glad you're on, Sister. Can you contact Mrs MacTaggart for me, please? Tell her I won't be home tonight.'

'Of course I shall. Is there anyone else you'd like to notify? Anything else I can do for you?'

He shook his head. 'Nothing, thanks. No one. No ties, you see.'

What a sad statement! 'Try to relax,' Patty said, 'I'll stay with you until Mr Callans decides what he's going to do.'

He nodded, then curled up as a spasm of acute pain again claimed him, just as the chief surgeon walked in, accompanied by Doctor Dykes.

'Now then, Ronnie, what's all this?' He was making an expert examination as he spoke, sure of what he was looking for.

'Sorry to take you away from your bridge, Henry — ouch!' Mr Simpson gasped as the probing fingers touched a sensitive spot. 'Had one or two twinges over the last few months, but thought — '

'Thought it would go away if you did nothing about it, eh? I won't say what you'd undoubtedly tell a patient who came up with that story! Well, luckily I'm available. We'll have you down to theatre right away. Get him prepped, Sister; Doctor, phone Theatre Three. When did you last eat, Ronnie?'

'Early morning. Couple of mouthfuls of tea only. Felt queasy.'

'Good, good.' He ordered the usual premedication. 'We'll find a bed for you in the private wing, Ronnie.'

'No!' Mr Simpson's voice came out strong. 'I'd prefer to stay here — if you can spare the bed, Sister? You'll be in charge this week-end, won't you?'

'Yes, I shall.' Her answer came unhesitatingly. She knew he must dread being helpless at the mercy of strangers. 'And if it's all right with you, sir,' she looked over at the chief, 'we'll certainly nurse you in here. It's a fairly quiet room and we can keep an eye on you very conveniently.'

Mr Callans nodded. 'I've no objections, Sister. Right, Ronnie, see you shortly.' He walked out with the young doctor and the two went into the dutyroom, Patty following. Mr Callans had routine orders to pass on, then took his leave, escorted to the doors by Doctor Dykes.

'I'm not happy about having him in here,' he remarked doubtfully, back with Patty.

'I should think he'll be a model patient,' she returned. 'We'll treat him exactly like everybody else. There's no time on this ward to give him any special attention beyond what his condition dictates — he knows he'd have got that in the private wing and he's refused to go there, so that's that! And you've got nothing to be worried about, you made the right diagnosis and everything should go normally.'

He nodded, mollified, then remembered, 'Weren't you supposed to be off this week-end?'

Patty nodded ruefully. 'That was the general idea. However, as you observed, I've just told Mr Simpson that I'll be on.' She shrugged. *'C'est la vie!'*

She checked that the students were on their evening routine and went back into the side room. Mr Simpson's eyes were closed, his face haggard.

'I'm going to prepare you for theatre now, Mr Simpson, but I'll disturb you as little as I can,' she said, and set to work to undress him. 'I know it can be unpleasant for medical staff to be hospitalised — we all think it can't happen to us — but as you know yourself, you'll pick up quickly once the op's over. You'll probably feel better than you've felt for months, and you'll soon forget all about your stay on Ward Eight.'

She kept talking quietly and reassuringly as she worked, as if he were a member of the lay public facing his first operation. The pre-med made him a little sleepy, and he looked almost comfortable by the time the theatre trolley came down the corridor and the attendants lifted him on to it.

Patty called the students into the dutyroom. 'Mr Simpson's an acute appendicitis, neglected, as you might expect of a surgeon! Abdominal pain, vomiting, rise in pulse rate, temp up nearly four degrees, history of 'twinges' as he calls them. He's going to be nursed in the side ward, so get the bed ready, please, before you do anything else. He should be up from theatre before we go off duty. Then check that the dressings trolley is properly set.'

She informed the office of the new arrival and notified the CNO that she'd be on duty after all that weekend, at which news she was reluctantly granted leave for an alternative date, always supposing she could make suitable arrangements with her staff nurse. Mrs MacTaggart was told that the dinner she was keeping hot for her employer would not, after all, be required by him, and why, and Patty promised to let the housekeeper know later in the evening how Mr Simpson was.

Then Patty sat back and contemplated her own problems. She'd phone the travel agency in the morning. There was no point in calling her mother; she'd told her in the afternoon that she was going abroad, so wasn't expected home anyway. It only remained to face the fact that she wouldn't see Dane tomorrow. Perhaps next week? The week after? She felt dejected after the recent burst of activity, and, somehow, the impetus that had brought her to the point of departure for Italy had gone.

With an effort, she closed her mind on personal feelings, scrubbed up, put on sterile gown and mask, and began the dressings, sparing a thought for Mr Simpson on the operating-table.

The surgeon came out of the anaesthetic in the recovery room and was awake, though drowsy, when he came back to the ward. Patty, in the middle of writing the day report, brought the report book through to the side room and got on with it while he lay dozing.

'Mr Callans did a nice job on you,' she remarked, as his eyes focused on her.

'Yes? Suppose it was just in time?' His voice was woolly.

'Exactly. He'll be telling you off about that, I expect, when you're feeling stronger.'

A ghost of a smile flitted across his face as he drifted into sleep.

'I'll be going off duty shortly,' she told him when his eyes opened again. 'Sister Cairns is on tonight — you know her, don't you?'

He nodded.

'And I'll be back on tomorrow. By that time you'll be feeling more human.'

When she left him he was sleeping peacefully, his colour good, with all the signs that his recovery would be uncomplicated.

'Don't envy you with Callans making the rounds,' Sister Cairns commented when Patty had taken the night report next morning.

'Never thought of that,' Patty admitted. 'Except he'll be watching his patient with an eagle eye.'

'He came in last night just before midnight to have a look at him. As everything seems to be going normally, I expect he'll soon delegate the visits to old Burgess.'

Mr Burgess was the other surgical registrar, and, even sooner than expected, after taking the ward round at record speed that morning, Mr Callans informed Doctor Dykes and Patty that from then on Mr Burgess would be filling in until Mr Simpson was back on his feet. 'And make that at your soonest, Ronnie,' he urged over his shoulder as he left.

Patty took the afternoon off, and the visitors' bell was ringing when she came back on the ward. Mr Simpson's door was closed. 'Any particular reason why?' Patty wanted to know.

'He has a visitor,' Staff Nurse Barry told her. 'A man. Mr Simpson was most anxious that he should be allowed to stay beyond visiting hour as he came in late.'

Patty sat down at her desk and was engrossed in paperwork until she heard the clatter of dishes from the kitchen and realised it was nearly time for the evening meal. It was about time, too, that Mr Simpson's visitor made himself scarce. She knocked at the door of his room and went in.

'Do you feel up to eating a light meal?' she said pleasantly to the surgeon, guessing that his visitor would take the hint. The man had his back to the door, and stood up at once, turning towards her. Patty gulped, and reached for the door handle to steady herself. 'Dane! How did you get here?'

For a second he stared at her, her astonishment mirrored in his face. Then 'Darling! Excuse us, Ronnie!' His arms were round her, her lacy cap was knocked awry as his lips came down on hers, warm, firm and demanding.

Patty pulled free at last, straightening her cap and smoothing down her dress. 'Excuse me, sir,' she said to Mr Simpson, her face crimson, her hair, she knew, straggling round her face. He was sitting back against his pillows, a satisfied smile on his face.

'Don't mind me,' he said mildly, and picked up a newspaper, ostentatiously hiding behind it.

'Dane, please, anyone could come in!' He was reaching for her again. Hot with embarrassment, she found herself at the same time aching to have his arms round her once more.

'Dearest, let them all come!' He kissed her again, and she responded fervently, then collected herself, and leaned away from him.

He conceded a return to convention and took a deep breath. 'Sorry, Patty, couldn't help myself . . . You asked how I happen to be here — might I ask you the same question? You wrote me you'd be off this week-end, and when I arrived and called your home, your mom said you'd flown off to see me! I expected that you'd be wandering around Naples at this very minute, hopefully in the company of a friend I'd briefed to take care of you if you turned up at the hospital.'

Patty glanced over at Mr Simpson to see if he was listening. He'd put his paper down. 'You cancelled your weekend leave for me, Sister?'

She fidgeted with the chart on the end of the bed. 'Well — I — you'd have been unhappy if I'd been off, and Dane didn't know I intended to go over to see him anyway,' she mumbled, quite

180

unable to think of a suitable excuse. 'But why did you leave Naples?' she demanded of Dane. 'Weren't you supposed to be lecturing this morning?'

'Patty.' He gathered her close once more, easily overcoming her initial resistance, and Mr Simpson rustled the paper understandingly. 'I re-scheduled the darn lecture. I couldn't spend another week away from you.' He was whispering in her ear.

'That's just how I felt!' she whispered, repressing an urge to giggle, and he hugged her so tightly she almost had to fight for breath. Her ears picked up the rattle of the trolley going into the ward with the cups and plates, and she struggled out of his grasp.

'I have to go.' She tried to anchor wisps of hair back under her cap.

'I, too.' He turned to Mr Simpson, tactfully ensconced again behind his paper. 'Goodbye, Ronnie, glad to see you're over the worst. Keep in touch!'

In the dutyroom he sat circumspectly in the chair at the side of her desk, mindful of the revealing window and the open door. 'Nearly forgot to mention, in the excitement of seeing you: as I had the car, I went to see your parents, and had a few minutes with Gerry, too. He's recovering most of his mobility, I was glad to see. A lot of it's due to his physical fitness, I think.

'After that I called Ronnie and heard he'd been forced to take some of his own medicine! So I came through here. Your pretty red-haired Welsh nurse very kindly let me in though visiting hour was nearly over.

'Ronnie said nice things about you.' He smiled at Patty's blush. 'I believe I have a case for feeling jealous! After all, he homed in on your ward when he felt bad, didn't he? He said you combined the skills of nursing with the loving kindness of a mother! I told him I had a perfectly satisfactory mom back in the States, and that I had a very different kind of relationship in mind with you!' He grinned wickedly.

'It never occurred to him apparently,

182

that I had no idea this was your ward. He presumed I knew. Anyhow, I was so busy telling him about the work I've been doing that he hadn't much chance to get a word in!'

'Oh, Dane,' Patty protested, smiling. 'How am I going to face him again after all this?'

'Darling, let's forget Ronnie, hospitals, patients and everything except you and me, just for one short evening. I have to get back tomorrow and we've wasted too much time already. When are you off?'

'Not till eight-thirty.'

'I'll be waiting at the main gate.' He glanced at his watch. 'More than enough time to see your chief surgeon and confirm the booking for my lecture in the spring. I'm beginning to feel I'm some sort of performer!'

'Well, theatres are your scene of operation!' He shook his head and groaned as he brushed her cheek with a finger, in farewell, and left the ward.

Patty carried the bright picture of

Dane's blue-eyed, tanned good looks in her mind as she helped the students through the evening chores, excitement mounting within her as the time drew near when she'd be alone with him, and when the phone rang at seven-thirty she answered it without the slightest premonition of disaster.

'Patty, Chris, Sister Casualty, here. We've had a couple of young boys in, knocked off their bikes by a hit-and-run driver. They're in theatre right now, but there's no room in the children's wards for them so they're going to be sent to you.'

Patty frowned. 'We have no empty beds, either.'

'There are spare cots in stores. The Assistant CNO's here just now and she says two are being sent up to you. Put them down the middle of the ward, she says. Sorry, Patty.'

'That's OK, Chris. What's the damage?'

'Multiple fractures: two legs, two arms. Lacerations. Better plan for drips, too, they're badly shocked. Best of British!'

'Thanks, Chris.'

Patty looked out the necessary bed linen, and when the cots arrived, set the two students to prepare them for the new arrivals, with cradles and drip stands. The patients were intrigued.

'A couple of kids, Sister? We'll need to watch our language!'

'I volunteer to tell them bedtime stories!'

'Keep him away from them, Sister! He'll corrupt the poor little beggars!'

They were silent, though, when the two trollies came in and the little figures were tucked up, bandages and plasters very much in evidence. Doctor Dykes followed them in and scrubbed up to insert the drip needles.

The children didn't look more than six or seven. One was white, the other a small Indian boy, and they both woke up quite soon. Patty was sitting beside the coloured child and Nurse Wilkes, the second-year student, at the cot of

185

the other, while the first-year student, Nurse Thomson, rushed around the ward whipping off the day covers and doing a final tidy around before the night staff came on.

'Hello,' Patty said as two big brown eyes swivelled round and fixed on her in a mixture of fright and bewilderment. 'You fell off your bike and now you're in hospital, but you'll soon be better.'

'Where's Jack?' His eyes was shining suspiciously, his lower lip trembling.

'Ask your patient if he's Jack,' Patty called to Wilkes.

'He's Jack,' she confirmed, 'and yours is Zak.'

'Jack's here and he's just fine,' Patty told the child. 'He's in bed, too, and you'll both be up and about quite soon. If you feel sore anywhere be sure and tell us and we'll try and make it better.'

This was all too much to grasp, and the tears finally brimmed over. He was sobbing quietly, Patty drying his face with a swab, when Nurse Thomson came to say that both sets of parents had arrived to see the boys.

As so often happened, the visitors upset the children even more, and when Zak's anxious father and mother took their leave, Patty sat down again beside him and held his uninjured hand, stroking it gently, and speaking softly of anything she could think of that might interest him: school and holidays, toys and treats.

Gradually he calmed down, but when she told him she had to go away for a few minutes, he grabbed hold of her hand and held it fast, his eyes pleading not to be left alone. Patty enlisted the help of one of the patients, a man with a young family, to sit by the boy while she did her ward round. 'I'll be back soon, Zak,' she promised, but as she walked away she heard him crying again.

Patty sighed. It wasn't easy to nurse children. Their helplessness was much more difficult to cope with than that of adults, and it was virtually impossible to get through to them that their present predicament wouldn't last. To them, hospital was alien country, the nurses and doctors enemies bent on inflicting pain, and they were haunted by the thought that they'd never be home with Mummy and Daddy again. She clearly remembered days on children's wards during her training, when she went home to cry all week-end for her small patients. Jack seemed to be a more sanguine little boy, and Nurse Wilkes had coaxed a smile out of him.

Patty concentrated on her round. Mr Simpson had been sitting on the side of his bed for a short time after supper, on the first stage of his recuperation, and looked up alertly as she went into his room.

'I saw the trollies rolling past,' he said. 'Emergencies?'

Patty told him about the children.

'Poor little fellows, they'll be miserable not knowing what's happening to them.'

Patty, checking his condition, was

pleased that he showed so much sympathy and understanding.

'You'll be trying to get off duty in good time,' he said, and she felt her face redden.

'Yes, Dane will be waiting for me.'

'It's not easy conducting a courtship when one's a nurse and the other's a doctor.'

'I'm discovering that.'

Sister Cairns came on. Zak's sobs had risen to a climax.

'What on earth?'

Patty explained about the new arrivals.

'Heavens, we're going to have some night if this keeps up!'

'I'll go down and see if I can soothe him — it's only one of them who's upset. I'll try and get him off to sleep.'

'I'd be grateful if you could do that, Patty. I'm short of a junior tonight and I certainly haven't anyone with time to sit by him.'

Zak was almost hysterical when she went up to his cot. She took his hand

and slowly his crying tailed off into hiccups and he lay gripping her hand desperately. She told him he had to lie very still until the doctors said his arm and his leg had mended. She pointed out that it was just like Daddy mending his toys. He listened, but held on tightly to her hand. She said he might be moved into a children's ward, but that even if he stayed here, she'd find some toys for him to play with.

It was after nine, and the night staff were working round them, but Zak had eyes only for Patty. She said, at last, she had to go home to bed, and would see him in the morning, and that elicited another bout of screaming. Dane would soon give up waiting and come to find her. What could she say? She couldn't leave this little fellow, not in the state he was in; she must see him fast asleep before she went off the ward.

Dane came in shortly after. She saw him walk up the corridor and knock at the dutyroom door, then stride into the ward. She indicated the child.

'Hi,' Dane said. 'How are you making out?'

The small boy squeezed Patty's hand with all his might, and Dane noticed it.

'He isn't going to let you go, darling,' he said in a low voice that couldn't be overheard. 'I wouldn't leave him if I were you. I'll wait in the doctors' home till ten. If you get away, phone me there. We might have a few moments together. If not, goodbye and God bless. I'll be over again in a few weeks' time. I'll be in Germany by then, and I'll call you the night before I leave, to check. No more taking chances. I love you, Patty, never forget that. I want you to be my wife. And I'm a very determined person.' He touched her cheek with the back of his hand and she watched him go with a feeling of deep despondency.

They both recognised the familiar trap, between what was seen as a duty towards a patient, and the call of private life. Both had made the choice long ago, and there was nothing to say but goodbye.

Zak was tiring, and Patty watched him fight the onset of sleep. Each time she eased her hand away he woke with a cry and held it again, until at last the silky eyelashes lay at rest on the babyish curve of the cheek, and his hand went limp. She sat for another few minutes to be sure.

'I'll pick up some books from the children's ward when I go for dinner,' Sister Cairns said, as Patty prepared to leave the ward at last. 'He should sleep soundly now, and he'll find something interesting on his locker when he wakes up. And I'll move the cots so that he and Jack can see each other. Thanks, Patty, you've been a great help.'

Although it was well after ten, Patty phoned the doctors' home on the faint chance that Dane was still there, but the doctor who answered said he'd left some time before.

Next morning the two boys — 'the

192

terrible twins' the patients had christened them — were off their drips. Sister Cairns had kept her word: the cots were parallel to each other, and there was a queue of up-patients waiting to play games with them or read to them.

Zak had given Patty only a passing glance — he had much more exciting company — and she wondered how he was going to react later in the day when the two boys were being transferred to a children's ward, from which two patients were being discharged.

Mr Simpson smiled warmly when she went in to see him, but made no mention of Dane. He'd shed a lot of his solemnity, and submitted equably to her ministrations. Perhaps, she reflected, he feels safe with me now that he knows about Dane.

Jane Anston, the physiotherapist, off duty, came in for a chat in the afternoon. Patty was glad to see her. Visiting hour was a good time for getting files up to date, but she gladly put them aside and asked Nurse Thomson to make tea.

'So, what's new?' they both asked at the same time, and laughed together.

'You first,' Patty said.

Jane considered. 'Very busy. Looking forward to an early autumn week's holiday. I fancy Yorkshire. Somewhere handy for bracing walks over the moors and for dropping in on places like York itself and those lovely little villages you find up there. You kept on your toes as ever? You rarely have time to chat when I come on my rounds.'

'All go, here. I have a week-end due and I'll go home, of course. I don't have your energy. I'll laze around and eat my head off.'

'Lucky you don't have to watch your weight. If I had as much walking to do on the job I'd be lazy too, when I was off — and might not have all this superfluous flesh.' She patted her thighs ruefully.

'How about Paul? Can you leave him with anyone?'

'I wouldn't enjoy my holiday if I did. No, wherever I go, Paul goes. He's an adaptable little chap and I love his company. How's Gerry, by the way? I hear that the American surgeon who operated on him was seen in Ward Eight yesterday!'

Patty hoped Jane didn't notice her change of colour. 'The grapevine's well up to date! Gerry's doing very well, thanks, and, yes, Mr Culver visited Mr Simpson yesterday. They're old friends.'

'Ah, yes, Mr Simpson. The word is that he's hidden away in your side room!'

'He's not really hidden — his door's usually wide open for anybody to see him. If he'd wanted the Garbo treatment he'd probably have opted for the private wing, where Callans offered to find him a bed, but he preferred to come here. An obvious compliment to Ward Eight's good nursing! He's a good patient, actually. Appendicectomy, I suppose you know? I think he's been suffering for months, but like a typical medic, did nothing about it. Probably accounts for that lean and hungry look. Now he's got rid of the thing, I shouldn't be surprised if he becomes fat and jolly!'

Jane hesitated. 'If he has no visitors — do you think he'd mind if I looked in on him? On a purely social basis, you understand?'

'Great idea. Hardly anyone comes to see him. Just let me check if he's awake and receptive.' She came right back. 'Go in, Jane, and cheer him up. I'm sure he's lonely.'

She smiled to herself as the door of the side room closed softly, and pretended not to notice Jane's heightened colour and bright eyes when she emerged after the best part of an hour.

Mr Simpson's recovery, surgically speaking, was unremarkable, though his behaviour was a surprise to the ward staff, all of whom, including Patty, fully expected him to keep to the seclusion of his room. Instead, as soon as he was able, he was to be seen in the ward or the day room, speaking to everyone, offering a ready ear for the nervous admissions, consoling the more ill patients, and congratulating those who had recovered.

He was useful, too, immediately on hand when one of the more adventurous young men fell out of bed while trying to reach something at the back of his locker, and dislodged both a drip needle and a drainage tube.

'We're going to miss you,' Patty was able to tell him with truth when he came to say goodbye.

'Thanks for everything, Sister,' he said formally, then grinned. 'I've learned a lot in Ward Eight. I shall give Miss Brendrith a good report, I promise you.'

'So you're not sorry you didn't go to the private wing?'

'No regrets. By the way, Sister, if you happen to be free any time next week, would you care to come out for another of Mrs MacTaggart's meals? She must be very frustrated after having only herself to cook for, for the last few days.'

'Thanks, sir, I'd like that. That last dinner was a real treat.' They fixed a date.

'I'm hoping Miss Anston will be able to come, too,' he said diffidently.

'Oh, good.' Patty was pleased. 'Jane will enjoy Mrs MacTaggart's cooking even more than I did — she has to do all her own catering.'

'Yes, so I gather,' he said quietly.

'It's simply a thank-you gesture,' she told Jackie later over lunch. 'He's a nice bloke. We all got to know him better while he was a patient than in weeks of visiting as a surgeon, when we were petrified in his presence. I'm sure you'll find a difference in him, too, when he comes back. He's had a bad time, losing his wife, then suffering this wretched appendix.'

'You always see the best in everyone,' Jackie said. 'Pity you doubted Dane, of all people. I haven't met him, mind you, but from what you tell me he looks like a Greek god and Robert Redford rolled into one. I'm almost envious. Even you couldn't call Ken good-looking.'

'Ken's a dear.' Patty rushed to the defence of Jackie's future husband.

'There you go! You even have to stick up for other people's fellas! I remember how you talked me into agreeing to get engaged to him.'

'Well, was I wrong? I thought you were ideally suited to each other — and you are!'

'You may be right, kid, time will tell.' Jackie was six months older than Patty and sometimes invoked her seniority. 'Ken's one of the best, I admit it. Hope your Dane is as good for you as Ken is for me. There might be problems, though, having a handsome husband!'

There was no malice in the remark. Jackie was a good friend. Even the best of friends, however, is no defence against accidents of circumstance, or, to put it another way, depending on one's beliefs, against the workings of destiny.

7

Summer was coming to an end. Patty noticed how untidy the plants in the borders were as she passed through the grounds on her way between the dining-room, the Sisters' home and the ward. The trees, however, remained in full leaf, the lawns still required their weekly trim, and a spell of golden days, with a suspicion of frost at night, had begun.

Her morale was high. Gerry's progress continued. He was up on his feet now, enthusiastically following his physiotherapist's instructions to the letter. His director of studies had visited him and given him a tremendous boost by promising him his place in the final year, although his physical participation would necessarily be curtailed. 'Because I did so well in the first two years,' he told Patty jubilantly during one of her regular visits.

He'd lost some weight and had the pallor of a long-term bed patient, although he was now out and about in the hospital grounds whenever he had the chance, but Patty could only marvel whenever she saw him that he'd come through the ordeal so well. He was missing the wages from his holiday job, and she discreetly passed him a contribution every time she saw him and promised to help him in kitting himself out for the start of term.

'I'll pay every penny back, Pat,' he would emphasise, kissing her affectionately, and she would hug him, loving him still more for his courage. Best of all, he would soon be home, and their parents were correspondingly happy.

Mr Simpson, though not yet back on duty, was fit. The dinner for Patty and Jane had gone off well. Jane had brought Paul, and had taken Patty along with them in her car, and Patty had quietly watched what she hoped would be a firm attachment taking root.

She recognised that she was there in the role of chaperone.

Several days afterwards, Jane confided with a blush that she and Ronnie had decided to join forces for a week in the Dales, he to convalesce, she to unwind. Paul and Ronnie, it seemed, had taken to one another, and the prognosis for a satisfactory alliance was good. She was happy for Jane and Paul, both, she felt, in need of a man in their lives, and thought Jane's unpretentious, down-to-earth quality was right for the surgeon. Jackie, put in the picture, was equally pleased.

Patty herself was looking forward with reservations to a visit from Dane. They'd been disappointed twice since the first mix-up, when accident cases had come in from German autobahns, and he'd been called in for consultation. She hid her frustration. This was a foretaste of life with Dane, when his work would come between them. As far as the forthcoming visit was concerned, she'd believe in it when she saw him.

The ward, even with Mr Simpson back, continued to struggle to keep up with its surgical lists. Operations classed as non-urgent had been put back while he was out of action, and now they jockeyed with emergencies for treatment, and the surgeon was frequently forced to discharge patients before they would normally have been allowed home, to continue their post-operative care in out-patients, in order to provide beds for acute surgical cases.

A young teacher, Tony Waldon, had been in the ward for some days, but there was no question of his being moved out. Tony's case, Mr Simpson told Doctor Dykes and Patty, was worrying. A fitness freak, he'd slipped on taking off for a back flip in the school pool and entered the water awkwardly. He'd had to be lifted out, and had been lying flat ever since, complaining of severe pain in the small of his back and down both legs.

'He admits he's had some pain in that region before. This accident was the last straw,' Mr Simpson said grimly. 'He's been abusing his body for years, ignoring aches and pains, and now it's caught up with him. Look at this — ' he pointed out a shadow on Tony's X-ray photograph. 'Frankly, we can't rule out a tumour, though it could be a disc that's ruptured. If it's a tumour — ' he frowned, ' — surgery is chancy at best. We're waiting to see if the next pictures show growth. Meantime, I've ordered a myelograph to check if the canal is clear.

'Really, the troubles these sportsmen bring on themselves! If they're not injured when they're young, they land up in the arthritis clinics when they're old! — Oh, sorry, Sister, I forgot — your brother. Though he's a professional; he's learnt to avoid most risks.'

Patty agreed with everything he said. She knew his anger was directed against the waste of youthful strength and energy, and that he felt deeply for all his patients. She was sorry for the man, too; he was in his early thirties and had no idea that his condition was causing so much concern, or, if he had, he didn't show it.

'Let's have the sports section, mate,' she heard him call across the ward as she went in on a morning visit, 'Ah, hello, Sister, how are you this fine morning?'

'I'm very well, thanks, Tony, but I hear from Sister Cairns that you had a bad night.'

'Nothing to worry about,' he said airily. 'Have to keep the night staff on their toes, you know! Can't let them sleep all night!'

'Mr Simpson has you down for a myelograph this morning. It probably sounds worse than it is.' She explained the injection into the spinal canal of a liquid that would show up on the X-ray screen.

'You suspect a blockage, then?'

He was too intelligent to be fobbed off with a lie, however well-intentioned. 'It's possible,' she said cautiously.

'So — an operation to clear it? Tricky area, eh?'

She nodded. His thin, clever face had clouded over. 'They'll only operate if it's going to help.'

He sighed. 'Hope they do and it will. I don't want to spend my life in a wheelchair, but if I have to, I shall.'

A lump came to Patty's throat as she thought of Gerry. 'It won't come to that,' she said, more confidently than she felt. Ronnie was more than competent — 'brilliant' she'd heard theatre staff say of him. Tony would get the best of treatment if surgery were required. You must be objective, she reminded herself, not for the first time. Becoming personally involved with a patient was just not on.

Tony returned from his myelograph to regale the ward with a mock-horror account of a lumbar puncture and the subsequent tilting up and down of the table he was strapped to, in order first to move the injected fluid up the spine, and then to bring it back down to be extracted. 'Great training for the roller coaster,' he recommended, 'and having it done in the dark certainly adds to the fun!'

His joking, Patty saw, hid a deep concern for his future, and she was relieved for his sake when Mr Simpson decided there was no tumour and that he'd do normal surgery for a slipped disc.

A ruptured one, he reported later. 'It had to be removed, of course. He must have suffered plenty over a period. The vertebrae on either side will eventually fuse together and he should have good mobility. Let's hope he gives back flips a miss from now on!'

Patty found herself spending more time with Tony than she usually gave to post-ops. He required careful turning from side to side at regular intervals, and attention to the side he'd been lying on. She was accustomed to hearing patients' personal problems, and Tony told her his in detail behind the curtains that gave a certain amount of privacy. She found the serious side behind the funny-man image he cultivated.

'Whatever state I'm in when I leave here, I'll go on teaching,' he said once. 'My folks have gone short to see their wonderful Anthony — I'm an only child, unfortunately — to see me get my degree. And I'm a good teacher, Sister. I'm aiming for head of department and the top of the tree. A very good marriage prospect, wouldn't you say?'

She settled him comfortably. 'Some girl's going to be lucky,' she agreed lightly.

'And it won't be me,' he finished for her, in falsetto, but there was no laughter in his eyes.

'I always wanted to marry a nurse,' he said on another occasion. 'Are you free, Sister, by any lucky chance? I think I'm falling for you!'

'Patients have a habit of falling in love with their nurses,' she returned. 'It's like holiday romances — as soon as you get home you'll forget all of us!'

'I shan't forget you, Sister. Are you married? Engaged? Living-in?'

'Engaged.' She was unwilling to discuss her private life with a patient, but couldn't evade the answer.

'Ah, there's many a slip!' he warned.

'You've slipped once too often, my lad, it's you for the straight and narrow when you get out of here!'

He managed to catch hold of her hand and planted a kiss on it before she tucked him up and pulled the curtains back, and she made sure that Nurse Barry or one of the students attended to him for the rest of his stay as a bed patient.

She couldn't avoid taking out his stitches, though. Mr Simpson had asked her to do it. Tony lay obediently still, trying to control the involuntary jump as she snipped each one. 'Mr Simpson's needlework is very neat,' she remarked. 'You won't be ashamed to show your friends your operation. This is the last one.'

'Thanks, Sister,' he said as she pulled the suture through and dropped the fragment of thread in a dish. 'I'd like to see you with your hair down — literally, I mean. Blonde, mm — lovely. Green-brown eyes. Will you come out with me when I'm through with Ward Eight?'

'No, Tony. You have to forget me. Get back to your own life and your own friends and look back on this as a brief interlude in your career. We'll have you out of bed tonight, and you can expect to be going home quite soon.'

He winced as she helped him to turn on his side, and she couldn't be sure that his expression hadn't shown an ugliness that was quite unlike him. She dismissed the thought. Tony was an even-tempered bloke, and had been a good patient; he was possibly showing a reaction to the apprehension felt by some patients at the prospect of stitches being removed, fearing more discomfort, or even pain.

When the time came for him to be discharged, Patty's mind was on more urgent matters: primarily, on her latest collection of pre- and post-op patients, and then, a poor second, on the bliss of seeing Dane the following week-end.

Off duty not long after five p.m. on the Friday, she went to the Sisters' home to change, and then back to the dining-hall for a light snack. Dane's call to confirm his visit was timed for seven p.m., after which she'd take the bus home to Farnton, a two-hour journey. Dane was to join her there next day.

The sun was beginning to dip behind the trees that surrounded the hospital when she came back out into the grounds, and she set off on the long way back, enjoying the clear air that already held the tang of autumn. In spite of the previous cancellations, she couldn't quell an inner exhilaration, and she followed the path through a thicket near the boundary fence and along past the back of the kitchens with a spring in her step.

It was between shifts, no one else was on the path, and, staring into nothing, her mind on the coming day, she found herself looking twice at a shadow beside the back door of the kitchen. Only on the second glance did she identify it as a small boy, sitting on the bottom step, sobbing to himself.

'Hello, what are you crying for? Are you lost?'

He looked up at her, the tears making tracks down his dusty cheeks. She sat down beside him. A baseball cap, too large for him, was balanced on hair bleached almost white by the sun, his eyes were blue, his skin tanned dark gold. He sniffed, the tears becoming fewer.

Patty found a tissue in her pocket and wiped his face. 'There, that's better! Blow!' He blew his nose. 'Oh, dear, you're a very sad little boy! Have you lost your mummy?'

He didn't answer. His shirt and denims were grimy. He looked about four, but he straightened his shoulders in a kind of defiance against the world, and Patty hid a smile.

'I think I've made a mistake, you're not a little boy at all, you're a big fellow. You must be — er, let me see — five or six?'

'Four,' he muttered. 'But I'm not a kid. I'm a very sens — sens — '

'Sensible?'

'Sensible guy for my age. My pop says so.'

Pop? She placed his accent.

'Do you come from America?'

He nodded.

'And have you come all the way here in a plane? By yourself?'

'With Heidi.'

'Oh. Who's Heidi?'

'She's Pop's girl-friend,' he said importantly. 'She looks after me. But she got lost,' the little voice quavered.

'Ah, now I've got the picture. We have to find Heidi, is that the problem?'

He nodded again, with a final sniff.

'Right, take my hand and we'll go straight up to the office and see if someone called Heidi is looking for her friend — what did you say your name is?'

'David.'

Not usually slow in the uptake, Patty could only make the excuse to herself afterwards for not immediately recognising who he was, that her mind was at the time centred wholly on Dane. She was recalling his voice, his face, his body, and her senses were dwelling on their meeting next day.

The small boy, obviously an independent soul, withdrew his hand from hers, but marched beside her, his head held up, his back like a miniature soldier's. They were on the slope leading up to the administrative block when a figure stepped from the entrance of one of the ward buildings into their path.

'Sister Henden, I presume,' said Tony Waldon, and took her into an imprisoning grip, his mouth fastening on hers in a bruising kiss. It was so unexpected, Patty could only submit, and she gasped for breath when he released her. There was a cruel smile on his face, and she flinched as he reached for her hair, which hung loose, and twisted the ends in his fingers. 'Mmm . . . just as I imagined it!'

Patty found her voice. Her initial shock was succeeded by a wave of fury. She pushed him violently away. 'Tony, get out of here before I call the security men and make an official complaint,' she snapped, a sense of outrage sharpening her voice.

' 'An official complaint',' he mimicked as he moved away, limping slightly, Patty noted — so he was still feeling the effects of his operation. She was shaking now in reaction as she watched him disappear in the direction of the main gates, and remembered the child.

David had run up the road ahead of her and was standing holding hands with a red-haired girl. He and Heidi seemed to have found each other. She walked towards them, aware that both had witnessed the little cameo with her and Tony, that her mouth was aching, and that she felt contaminated. She tried to smile.

'Hi,' said Heidi. 'You found my boy for me. Thanks.' She was American too, older, close up, than she appeared from the distance, with a cheerful freckled face and close-cropped curly hair.

'Glad you two got together. The hospital's a big place.'

'It certainly is. I was enquiring after one of the Sisters and left this rascal outside for a moment. Seems he was interested in exploring the grounds and went off without me. But all's well that ends well.'

'Perhaps I can help you to find your friend?'

'Sure, perhaps you could, at that.' She consulted a scrap of paper. 'Sister Patty Henden, Ward Eight? Only she's gone off duty for the week-end and no one knows where she is right now.'

'I'm Patty Henden.' Patty was utterly confused.

'You are?' She eyed up Patty's jeans and sweater. 'Well, of course I expected to see you in uniform! I'm Heidi West.' She held out her hand. 'Delegated by one Dane Culver to find you and deliver this bundle of mischief to you — his son, David. He said you'd know all about him.'

Dane's son? 'But why — how — ?'

'Dane's been called to somewhere in Norway. Some offshore accident on an oil rig. He's not due in Scandinavia for weeks, but they put in a special request, and as you'll understand, if you know Dane, he couldn't refuse. He's actually in transit at this very time and I've been getting panicky about finding you 'cos he impressed on me that his call to you tonight was timed for seven.'

Patty felt herself drooping. 'So he won't be over here this weekend?'

'Sorry, impossible.' The girl's pretty face was sympathetic. 'I know how you feel, honey. I'm a medic myself and there's no way I can plan for anything without a get-out clause.'

'But David?'

'Dane said he'd warned you about

him.' Dimly, Patty recalled a sentence in Dane's last letter — 'I've got a surprise for you!' This was the surprise? The child was looking anxiously at her. She recovered quickly.

'Of course he did, and I'm so glad you've managed to come, David, although your dad — Pop — can't make it. Er — what arrangements have you made?' she asked Heidi.

'Well, you don't know how I come into the picture, do you? I brought David over from LA last week to see his father. Dane had found a little German girl to be with David while he was working. I'm on a study tour in Europe and Dane inveigled me into taking David with me this week-end to the UK as he wasn't going to get here. It's all so mixed-up, isn't it, but the bottom line is that I have a couple of engagements lined up and he's hoping you can cope with David until I pick him up on Sunday and get him back to Bonn. Can you unravel that little puzzle?'

'Quite clear now. I'll take David home with me — is that OK with you, David?' The boy, listening with a worried look, nodded, obviously relieved. Poor little chap, being passed from one minder to another, and probably homesick for his mum as well. 'And if you can be at the hospital on Sunday late afternoon I'll have him ready to go back to his pop.'

Patty walked with them to Heidi's car and took charge of a small week-end bag for David, collected her own case, and they went for the bus. Now that his immediate future was secure, the little boy chattered away without a stop. Patty longed to ask him about his father and mother and Heidi, but soon found there was no need: he was a fount of unsolicited information, and had some questions for her.

One of his first was disconcertingly frank: 'Is that man who kissed you your boy-friend?'

Patty shuddered at the memory of Tony. 'No, no — he's — he was a patient. I'm a nurse,' she tried to explain; 'I look after the sick people in hospital and help to make them better. That man has been ill but now he's well again.'

He digested that for a moment. 'My pop doesn't kiss the people he makes better. He kisses his girl-friends. He kisses Heidi. She's his best girl; he said so. I think she's OK. She's a doctor like my pop. I wish she would marry him. Then I'd get to live in his house all the time. He takes me to good places and I get hot dogs and burgers. My mom doesn't let me eat hot dogs or Coke or — j — junk food.'

Patty listened with the feeling she was eavesdropping.

David looked with interest at the changing scenery. 'I wouldn't like to live here, no one has a pool, Heidi says, and they don't play baseball or basketball. I'm going to make the school team when I start school. Pop says I'm good enough.

'He's going to take me to all the big

games in the fall and I'll get burgers and things for lunch.' He went off at a tangent. 'My mom has lots of boyfriends. She says I'm not to tell Pop, but I can tell you, can't I? Uncle Hugh bought me a baseball bat, it's pretty good. Uncle Sid said he'd get me a snorkel set, but he forgot. Maybe Pop will give me that for my birthday. Is Pop going to marry you?'

Patty was no longer certain. 'Perhaps. He'll tell you himself, won't he?'

'I like you,' he said, giving her a quick inspection. 'Will you come back to LA and live with Pop and me?'

'But you live with your mom, don't you?'

'Um. Sometimes. Sometimes I live with Pop. When he's on vacation. He calls me when I'm at Mom's.'

It was a glimpse into the divided world of the child of divorced parents. David appeared to take it in his stride, getting the best out of both mother and father, but many children must suffer unspoken insecurities as they're shunted from one household to another.

Patty, however, was less concerned with the social problems into which her small companion had been thrust, than with her own twin fears: would Heidi, or, more likely, David, report to Dane that they'd seen her in that apparently passionate embrace with Tony? And was Heidi, indeed, Dane's girl-friend? Despising herself, she had to ask, 'Do you see Heidi when you're at home?'

'Heidi lives in Pop's hospital,' he said scornfully, as if she should know all about it. 'She's his girl-friend. I told you. She's going to take me back home to Mom soon. In a big plane.' He nodded. 'It flies over the ice and snow. Have you seen any snow? Pop said there's snow where he's gone — to — Sc — Scan — '

'Scandinavia.'

He nodded. She saw that his eyelids were closing. It was warm in the bus. He tried to keep awake. She drew him over to her and held him against her as he finally slept, seeing Dane in the shape of his face and that self-confident air, loving the child as she yearned for the father.

'What a lovely surprise!' Mrs Henden hid her astonishment as her daughter walked in with a small friend, and produced her typically warm welcome.

'This is David, Dane's son.'

'Indeed! I know your daddy, David. What a clever doctor he is! You must be very proud of him!' The little boy's cheeks flushed and he smiled shyly.

'I can see you're sleepy, David, so we'll keep all the talking for tomorrow, shall we? Now, where shall we put you to sleep? Gerry's room's all ready for Dane,' she said to Patty, who shrugged wearily.

'Put him in there.'

'Dane's cancelled again!' It was a statement rather than a question.

Mrs Henden turned her attention to the child. 'Let's get you something to eat then you can go off to bed and we'll see what fun we can have in the morning. How about a glass of warm milk and some chocolate chip cookies?'

He drained the glass, ate four biscuits, and looked enquiringly at Patty.

'Bed?' she suggested, and he nodded. Teeth brushed, blue and white striped pyjamas on, he looked like a little cherub. He climbed into bed and closed his eyes. Patty tucked the covers round him, blew a kiss into his hair, and turned out the light. She went downstairs, where her mother, all alone, sat waiting for her, and burst into tears.

Mrs Henden passed over a box of tissues and Patty stopped sobbing, blew her nose and wiped her face.

'Sorry, Mum, I seem to regress twenty years when I come home.'

'No need to apologise, dear. If you can't show your feelings in your own home, where else? I know how disappointed you are that Dane's not coming after all. But tell me how you come to have David in tow. Dad's away round to the man next door. They're planning a golf tournament and I expect he'll have supper there, so we can talk girl talk for an hour or two.'

Patty took a deep breath and selected her words. 'Mum, this isn't the first time I've been in love — or thought I was. But it's the first time I've been so unhappy about it, and that can't be a good sign for the future. It's always going to be like this — Dane's professional obligations will keep spoiling our plans, and I can't cope with that, I just can't. Besides — I don't feel sure of him any more.' She told her mother about Heidi and what David had said about her, and Mrs Henden shocked her by laughing.

'Honestly, darling, I can't believe that you'd take the word of a child of that age! What does he know about his father's true feelings for Heidi? You seem determined to put the worst possible interpretation on everything Dane does — first there was Donna, now Heidi. And what has he done? He's bound to know other women just as you know other men, but it surely doesn't mean that he's contemplating matrimony, or any other relationship, with every one of them?'

'But they're all such glamorous creatures! I haven't seen Donna but I know what Dane thinks about her, and Heidi is a doctor and fearfully attractive. How can I compete?'

'Patty, I can't listen to any more of your nonsense. You have a beautiful face and hair and a perfect figure. And you're the most caring person I know. Don't you think Dane appreciates all that?'

'You're prejudiced, Mum, all mothers are about their children. I know Gerry has the good looks in this family, and as for being caring, that's not a quality anyone falls in love with, although I suppose it could come in useful one way or another. And Dane is so utterly gorgeous. How did he come to look at me at all?'

Mrs Henden sighed. 'Look, Patty, ask yourself one question: how would you feel if Dane wrote to you that he was getting married to Heidi, so goodbye?'

'Shattered,' Patty owned.

'There you are, then. You truly want him, so you're going to have to be patient. He has to complete this year, you know that very well. Then you'll get together and work everything out. After what he did for Gerry, I refuse to listen to anything bad about Dane, so let's forget this latest piece of bad luck for you, which may mean the difference between life and death for someone else, and concentrate on giving little David a happy week-end; he's been neglected even more than you.'

It was easy to bring smiles to the boy's face. Patty's father was full of suggestions to please Dane's son, but in the end, Patty and her mother sent Mr Henden off to golf and took David to a week-end fair, where he enthusiastically spent the £5 Mr Henden gave him on rides and sideshows.

In the afternoon they visited Gerry, finding him surrounded with rugby pals, and in good humour. They made their visit short to give him the opportunity of talking to his mates, and spent the rest of the day at the coast, the highlight of David's day being tea at the local burger place.

'Gee, I've lots to tell Pop,' he said happily as Patty tucked him up in bed, a small pile of treasures acquired during the day carefully set out on his bedside table. 'I like it here,' he confided. 'I like you. I think maybe Pop should marry you. Instead of Heidi.' His eyes were heavy. 'P'raps . . . ' Patty kissed him, suddenly filled with hope that David's 'perhaps' might, after all, come true.

8

David knocked at Patty's door on Sunday morning long before the time she usually got up. Hair tousled, bright and chirpy, he made himself comfortable on her bed and asked eagerly what they were going to do that day.

'Is the sun shining?' Patty asked sleepily.

He bounded over to the window and pulled back the curtains. 'The sun's shining on a spider's web,' he reported, examining the creeper that grew round the window. 'It's got drops all over it. Like Mom's sparkly ring. And there's silver water on the grass.'

'That's dew.' Patty abandoned plans for a long lie in. 'Let's go to the park. Would you like that — swings, climbing frame, slides?'

'Great!'

'Right, a quick shower and we'll get

dressed and have breakfast.'

She left a note for her parents, still asleep, to say they were off to Linton Park and would be home for lunch, and she and David set out into a summer landscape, the sky cloudless, the air warming up.

The walk to the park took nearly twice as long as usual, as David paused to observe things of interest to him on the way, asking innumerable questions, and when they found the playpark, Patty was glad to sit down on a bench and watch him rush from one play installation to another.

'Shall we visit the museum?' she asked him when, at last, he appeared to tire. 'Have you ever been to a museum?' The Shearton Gallery was nearby.

'Oh, yes.' He jumped up. 'Pop takes me to museums. Lots of old things.'

'We could go for a drink as well — are you thirsty for a Coke or a glass of orange juice?'

'Coke, please!' He pulled her to her feet impatiently.

In the gallery, he walked beside her, looking intently at the various exhibits, speaking quietly, careful not to touch anything, and after a short inspection, before he had time to become bored, they went down to the cafeteria.

Later, she took the chance of a quick glance round the pictures, trying to spot pieces brought from the store of thousands to take their turn on view. David had become engrossed in a Chinese Buddha figure, larger than himself. There was unaccustomed quiet. It was too early for many visitors.

She reached the Virgin and Child. Patty looked up at the picture, remembering the last time she saw it, trying to see herself as Dane had seen her in that serene face. The baby balanced confidently on his mother's lap. A happy mother and child with no apparent premonition of events to come. Patty sighed . . . then jumped as a shriek rang round the gallery.

'Pop!' David's shout shattered the silence. Patty whirled round to see him flinging himself into Dane's arms. The man lifted him up and kissed him lovingly, then came over to her. 'Darling!' His other arm brought her close, and the three of them stood in an embrace that was broken when David began to wriggle free.

'Darling,' Dane said again, and this time, unencumbered, he was able to kiss her, long and ardently, to let her go and kiss her again. 'I thought I might find you here when your mother told me you'd gone to the park.'

The little boy was watching solemnly. 'Is Patty your girlfriend, Pop?'

'She certainly is.' Dane took the child's hand and Patty's arm and turned to leave.

'Are you going to marry her?'

'I most definitely am. OK with you?'

'OK with me, Pop. I like her. She took me to the swings and bought me a Coke and a doughnut.'

Patty heard the words through mists of unreality. This couldn't be true. Dane — here? The dialogue went on.

'And we went to the fair. And I had a burger . . . Patty kissed a man. But he wasn't her boy-friend. He was sick and got better,' he threw in irrelevantly, and Patty caught her breath. David went on, 'The ocean here only has baby waves. Why is that, Pop?'

Patty shot a look at Dane. He gave no sign of having taken any notice of the remark about herself, and was already answering the following question. The treble and baritone voices formed a pleasing duet, Dane kept his firm hold of her arm, and Patty drifted out of the gallery and into the car as if in a dream.

Over the lunch table Dane explained his unexpected appearance. He'd completed his examination, escorted the patient back to land by helicopter, and into hospital, and flown to London on the evening plane. 'Stayed there overnight so that I could leave by road first thing this morning.' To David he said, 'You and I will drive Patty back to the hospital this afternoon, pick up Heidi, and head back to London for the plane to Germany. How does that sound?'

'Why do we have to pick up Heidi? Why can't Patty come instead?'

Dane ruffled his son's blond hair in smiling resignation. Mr and Mrs Henden, grasping the situation, offered to take David to a children's museum in the town for an hour or two, and it was only then that Patty and Dane were able to talk. He was sprawled on the settee and opened his arms to her. She curled up in his lap like a contented cat.

'At last!' He kissed her lingeringly, and ran his fingers through her hair. 'You can't think how I've longed for this moment! I can't live without you, Patty, that's what it amounts to, not even till the end of this endless year. I think of you all the time. It's wrecking my concentration.

'I used to enjoy my work, now I can't bear to face another day or another lecture room knowing you're so far away, and I've made up my mind: you must come over and join me. I thought it wouldn't be practicable, but I can't wait. We can get married over there if you like, in Germany, or France or Norway, wherever you decide. Just come over. Soon, please; please make it soon. I'm pining away without you . . . '

Snuggled into him, her head against his shoulder, she listened as he spoke of his plans for a honeymoon in Sorrento. He was sweeping her away in a heady rush of excitement, but a cold sickness that she couldn't ignore was growing inside her. Dearly as she had longed to be with him, never, in her most passionate thoughts, had she envisaged leaving the hospital before he left Europe, to marry him.

She had seen herself flying out to join him in California when he'd settled back home again, had pictured their wedding, with Gerry as his best man and Jackie her bridesmaid. In-built all the time, however, was the knowledge of the obligation she had to fulfil before she was free to take the happiness that marriage to Dane represented.

Two years before, the family had

been forced to instigate a ruthless economy drive. Holiday plans had been scrapped, the car had been sold; new clothes were out. The house was still mortgaged, and although Mr Henden had acquired a company car with the new job, he frequently commented that he'd rather have the extra salary and pay his own travelling expenses. Even now, every household bill was a minor trauma, there was little left over for luxuries, and no way that Gerry's final year could be financed without her help.

She couldn't tell Dane that they were living from hand to mouth — it wouldn't be fair to her parents; they'd suffered enough, and were still suffering. She couldn't begin to explain that Gerry's future — a future that Dane had made possible — was dependent on her. If she lost him, so be it . . .

'Well, what do you say?'

She'd missed his last words. 'Sorry, I was miles away.'

'I said, how much notice do you have to give?'

'Notice? Oh. I — er — I'm not sure. A month, perhaps — two months.'

He looked at her sharply, and she flushed, knowing he'd sensed her hesitation in making the instant commitment he was taking for granted would come from her. There was a long, uneasy pause. 'Am I right in thinking that you don't wish to join me?' There was an edge to his voice.

'I do want to be with you, Dane but — it's not so easy.' Even to her ears it sounded lame and insincere.

'Anything can be done if you really wish to do it.' His arms slackened and she slipped off his knees to sit beside him, staring out at the garden. The sun still shone but the room had chilled.

'What's the problem? Perhaps you've met someone else? What was it David said: he'd seen you kissing 'someone who wasn't your boy-friend' — perhaps you told him so? Be frank with me, Patty, please. I can take it. Is it all over between us? Was it just a summer romance? Have I been reacting all along like an emotional teenager?'

Her voice was hardly audible, her eyes were fixed on the carpet. 'There's no one else,' she said woodenly. 'I'm just — just not ready. It's too — too soon.' What more could she say? How else could she put it?'

'I see.' He stood up and moved over to the patio windows, his back to her. 'I guess I got it all wrong. Too impulsive, as usual. Thought we matched up so well. Thought you wanted me the way I wanted you. Nearly made another mistake, didn't I?' His tone was bitter.

'Youngsters may dither. Women of your age, Patty, know their own minds. You're trying to make it easy for me to accept that I have to stop thinking of you, aren't you? I'll try not to hold it against you. I'm not sorry we met, only sorry it didn't work out..I'll wait in the garden until your parents come back and then we'll leave.'

David's chatter when he returned

took up everyone's attention, and only Mrs Henden, sensitive to Patty's moods, noticed her pinched face and saw the bleakness in Dane's eyes when they said their goodbyes and left for Westingham.

Patty, her heart icy, endured the journey with a taciturn Dane and a vociferous small boy. When they reached the hospital she directed Dane to the office. Before they could get out of the car David spotted Heidi on her way to meet them, and Patty quickly said a formal goodbye to Dane, whose cold eyes swept briefly over her.

David had pursed his lips for a kiss from her, and she bent down to the little boy, returning his affectionate gesture. His arms went round her neck, hugging her to him for a moment, and by the time she'd disentangled herself, Heidi was upon them.

'Hi, you guys!' Unself-consciously she kissed Dane and leaned over to the back to David, who turned his face away to ask Dane petulantly, 'Why didn't you kiss Patty goodbye?'

As Dane drew breath to answer his son, Patty lifted her case and scrambled out of the car. She forced a smile to Heidi, waved quickly to the group, and walked purposefully towards the nearest ward block without looking back. A tumult of emotions was raging inside her, the overriding one being an urgent desire to give up nursing forever . . .

★　★　★

Routine continued in Ward Eight despite Sister Henden's inner despair; years of responsible nursing ensured that Patty's professionalism never wavered. Jackie was off on leave, and Patty missed her, getting through the first week by the simple expedient of thinking of nothing but her patients.

Staff Nurse Barry was her usual competent self, and Patty, leaning on her just a little, thought, not for the first time, of the loss to nursing her departure was going to be.

Jane Anston stopped at the dutyroom one afternoon after her ward work to report on her week with Ronnie. 'Really good,' she said. 'The three of us got on so well. Ronnie doesn't talk down to children. He treats them as equals, and Paul reacted by looking on him as a sort of big brother.

'In fact, he actually asked me if I was going to marry Ronnie! When I explained that the man usually asks the lady, and that the two people have to know each other really well before that happens, he said: 'I think you and Ronnie need to get together. I ought to have a father figure in my life, and he'd make a jolly good one! And you could have another baby — a brother or sister for me. It's not good for me to be an only child!'

'I don't know where he picked up the amateur psychology! At school, I expect. There are so many divorces these days, the children probably discuss their problems with each other.'

Jackie returned, full of plans for her

wedding, and it wasn't until their second lunch together that she casually asked if Patty had heard from Dane. She was dismayed to hear the story, and annoyed with her friend.

'You mean to tell me you let the poor man go back to Germany thinking you'd changed your mind?'

'What could I say?' Patty said miserably. Jackie knew all about the Henden family's financial problems. 'Could I tell him that I couldn't afford to marry him and leave my job? He might have felt obliged to fork out himself for Gerry and that would have been quite unacceptable for all of us. I told him I still loved him, but he assumed I was trying to let him down gently.

'There's nothing else I could have done, you must see that. In any case, he has someone already and the whole thing's off. I'll just have to forget him. We scarcely knew each other, anyway, we hardly had a chance to be together; just ships that pass in the night.'

'Oh, come on, Patty, don't be such a wet blanket! There's still a chance. He has to come back here eventually for his lecture date. Maybe, by then, he'll see things differently, and by that time Gerry's course will be nearly over.'

'Let's not talk about him any more,' Patty said firmly. 'I've got other things on my mind. District nursing, for one. It's about time I got out of Westingham General. If you and Ken start a family you'll be leaving, and I'll have no one here.'

'You'll still have Jane. Even if she and Ronnie Simpson get hitched, she'll keep on her job, I should think.'

'Maybe,' said Patty, and they left it at that.

★ ★ ★

She hadn't yet broken the news to her family, and put off going home, spending her days off walking and reading, until her next weekend's leave was due. Gerry was back home, and Mr

243

Henden had booked a table at a restaurant in town for a meal on the Saturday night to celebrate his recovery. Patty decided to keep her affairs to herself until the next day, and found herself fielding awkward questions. She hadn't realised the place Dane had already taken in the life of the family.

'Any chance of Dane making another visit this week-end?' her father asked hopefully.

'He's completely tied up,' Patty told him, finding it difficult to lie.

'Where is he now?' Gerry wanted to know. He was in high spirits. 'I wish he could see me properly on my feet. It would give him confidence for his next operations.'

Mrs Henden laughed. 'Dane's not short of confidence! He couldn't do the work he does if he had any doubts about his capabilities. Has he left Germany, Patty?'

'No, he'll be there for some time yet, then he goes to Scandinavia.' Patty remembered the schedule. 'Then to

244

France and Spain.'

'Have you made any decision yet about the date for the wedding?' her mother asked.

'Far too soon to think about it. Dane's mind's on his lectures. We'll have to wait till the spring before we plan anything.'

'Did I tell you I got a letter from Charlie last week?' Gerry said. 'She's saving up to come over here again next year! She's working in a supermarket after school and on Saturdays and Sundays, packing people's shopping in carrier bags. A mindless job — you only have to remember to put the squash-ables and breakables on top. But jolly well paid. When I go out to stay with you and Dane I shall try to pick up a spare time job, too. Charlie's going to investigate. You should have official permission but she says there are ways and means.'

Several of the diners in the restaurant knew Gerry and went over to their table to wish him well, and the occasion became even more festive when the proprietor, learning the reason for the outing, presented the family with a bottle of champagne.

Next morning they all slept late, though Mrs Henden was already busy in the kitchen when Patty went downstairs. She braced herself to tell her mother that she and Dane had parted, but it was impossible to say the words, they hurt too much. She ate the breakfast put in front of her, tasting nothing. Somehow, although it was weeks since he left, the wound had reopened. She wouldn't break down again, she told herself sternly, her mother had seen her in tears too often; it was time to apply adult restraint on her far too volatile emotions ... The resolution was short-lived.

'You look worn out, dear,' her mother said, and at the kindly words the waiting tears massed in her eyes.

'It's Dane, isn't it? I thought you and he had had some sort of misunderstanding while he was here. Haven't you sorted it out?'

Patty shook her head. 'There's nothing to sort out. We're finished. It's over. No use talking about it. It wasn't a misunderstanding, it was a mistake.'

'Did Dane say it was a mistake, or is that your opinion?'

'He said so. And there's someone else.' More tears. Would she never grow up?

'Well you must have said or done something most unlike you to make him turn against you to the extent of walking out like that.' Her mother's voice was no longer sympathetic, and Patty at once felt on the defensive.

'It wasn't altogether my fault, you know . . . Or, perhaps it was. I don't know. But I'm trying to forget Dane, so, Mum, please don't keep on about it.'

'But I shall keep on about it, Patty, because, whatever has happened, I have to say that I'm entirely on Dane's side in this instance. You see, no matter what you say about another girl, I know he loves you. I'm not altogether sure, though, that you're grown-up enough truly to love him!'

'Mum, how can you say that? I've confided in you all along. You know how I feel about him. How can you say that Dane loves me more than I love him?'

'Patty, you've told me about your love for him, certainly, but I haven't seen any signs of it in your treatment of him.'

'What do you mean?'

'I mean this: Dane is an eminent surgeon. Although we call him so casually by his first name, we — your dad and I — are fully aware of his position in the medical field. We know how much this year is costing him in expenditure of time and skill, and the effect it must be having on his emotions, also that he's paying every penny of his expenses out of his own pocket.

'I may say Charlie told us a lot more about him that she heard from her uncle, Mr Simpson, than we've gathered from either you or Dane. But you seem to regard him as just another boy-friend, to be treated whatever way the mood takes you, without any thought for his feelings. And, as I said, I know he loves you.'

'How do you know that?' Patty was reeling under her mother's criticism. 'What makes you think he doesn't look on me as just another pretty face — if you could call me pretty? Remember, he's divorced — why, do you suppose, his wife divorced him? We may never know, but isn't there just the faintest possibility that it was because he can't resist the women around him? Heidi is a typical example. You laughed when I told you what David said about her. But don't you think it may well be true?'

'Patty, we weren't going to mention this to you, but I think your father would agree with me that you should know about it.'

'About what?'

'Your dad wrote to Dane after

Gerry's operation, to thank him. He doesn't often write personal letters, I don't have to tell you that, and this was a rather special one, not altogether grammatically correct, perhaps, but sincere and from the heart.

'He told him how happy we were when first you, then Gerry, arrived in the family circle, and how we'd watched the two of you grow and develop, and how vulnerable we felt, as parents of two such dear children. Sounds pretty maudlin to you, perhaps, but it was how we both felt at the time of Gerry's accident, and still feel. Probably always will.'

'Mum!' Patty put her hand over her mother's on the table, and blinked back the tears.

'We do adore you both, you know. Or I hope you know; it's not easy to say, is it? You'll have the same feeling when you have children of your own. It's a happy burden — you worry about them when they're young and you worry about them when they're grown-up.

Shouldn't wonder if we don't agonise over the grandchildren, too, when they come!'

They both laughed shakily.

'What I want to tell you is that Dane wrote us a letter in return. We decided not to show it to you or Gerry, it was so obviously for our eyes alone, but I feel the time has come to let you read it.' She went to a drawer, took out an airmail envelope, and passed it over the table.

Almost against her will, Patty unfolded the flimsy sheets, covered with Dane's large distinctive writing, feeling she was an intruder. The words sprang out at her.

He thanked her parents first for their letter. 'I understand perfectly how you feel about Gerald and Patricia, believe me I do. My son David is forever in my mind, and I ache somewhere inside every minute he's away from me. The thought of losing him altogether is quite unbearable.

'But to thank me for saving Gerry's

active life is to attribute to me powers I do not possess, and, no matter how long I study — and I'm still learning — will never have. I am only a vehicle for the work of a far greater surgeon, and I rejoice as much as you do that the operation I performed has put a fine young athlete back on course for a long and fulfilled life.

'As for your daughter — ' Patty could hardly bear to read on; she was more moved than she had ever been in her life before. ' — I beg your forgiveness for loving her as I've never loved a girl before. I ask you to forgive me, because I'm going to take her away from you, and that's going to be a continual sorrow for you.

'Perhaps I can soften the blow by promising to care for her for the rest of our lives as you would wish her to be cared for, and by guaranteeing that our visits to you and yours to us will be numerous enough to ensure you are kept fully in touch with every aspect of our daily living . . . '

Silently, Patty refolded the letter. Her mother put the envelope back in the drawer and began to clear the table.

'Take a walk, Patty,' she advised. 'You don't want Dad and Gerry to find you like this.'

She walked blindly, Dane's words echoing and re-echoing in her brain as though he'd spoken them aloud. How could she have let him go as she did? And yet, what could she have said? He was so eager, so sure of himself and of her — what had she done to him? Hurt him abominably, that's what. How could she repair the damage? He had his pride, would he ever speak to her again? And if she had the chance to talk, what could she say? The thoughts revolved incessantly with no beginning and no end. She hadn't told her mother the true reason for the split, and would never be able to do so.

She had to keep up the pretence over lunch that all was well with her and Dane, grateful that her mother said nothing, and went back to the hospital with no solution in sight, to be involved at once in the Sisters' lounge in the discussion of a particularly juicy piece of gossip.

'Oh, Henden, have you heard the latest about our respected senior surgical registrar?' she was greeted as she looked in on the off-chance that Jackie hadn't gone out with Ken. One of the theatre Sisters was on the warpath.

'Mr Simpson?'

'The same. 'Ronnie' to his intimates. You're in surgical, you know that holier-than-thou attitude he takes to us Sisters. Well, what do you think? The great Mr Simpson has feet of clay! There's a report that he's been seen in a highly compromising situation with a member of staff of Westingham!'

Jane's blown her cover, was Patty's first thought. She must find out what she could and put her friend on her guard. 'How compromising?'

'They were seen in a small hotel in the wilds of Yorkshire. Just the sort of place to go when one's up to no good!'

'Perhaps they'd just gone in for a drink?'

'No way. They went upstairs together. Now, Mr Simpson was off for two or three weeks, right? It only remains to find out who had leave during that period and put one and one together. You haven't been to Yorkshire lately, have you, Henden?'

Patty managed a laugh. 'Not me! And I can't think offhand of anyone else. Sure it was someone from the hospital?'

'My informant says the face was familiar but she can't place the woman. Maybe it was a student — if so, all the worse for him! And we'll find out! Can't let him get away with lording it over us as if he wouldn't touch a nurse with a barge-pole, then carrying on behind our backs!'

They're sick, Patty thought, escaping to her room. They have nothing else to think about. The Sister who seemed to be conducting the witch-hunt was a notorious scandalmonger, and Patty fervently hoped Jane wouldn't be identified. Apart from the fact of spoiling the innocence of the holiday — if they'd intended to share a room, Jane wouldn't have brought Paul along — it was a nasty slur on Jane's professional reputation that would be difficult to erase. Gossip tended to stick, however out of line it proved to be. Luckily the tale-bearer hadn't seen the boy.

★ ★ ★

Jane came to the ward next day, saving Patty from trying to contact her, and she looked starry-eyed. 'Patty, congratulate me, Ronnie and I are engaged!'

'Jane, how marvellous! I'm so glad for you. I'm sure you'll be very, very happy together! You both deserve a lot of happiness.'

'Thanks, Patty. We're getting married quite soon, a very small, quiet wedding. We're not announcing the engagement, too much talk in the hospital; we'll put a notice in the local newspaper after we've tied the knot. Oh, Patty, I'm so excited! You'd think it was the first time! And Paul's over the moon. I'd never thought of marrying again, was never tempted, and now I feel I've been waiting for Ronnie all these years.'

Patty warned her about the sighting in Yorkshire. 'They're like terriers after a bone, they won't let up until they find out who Ronnie's companion was.'

'Imagine anyone spotting us!' Jane was surprised. 'It was such a lonely little place! Only three or four people staying there, and the occasional tourists dropping in for a drink. It must have been one of the casuals.

'Of course I can understand the determination to throw some muck. Ronnie does tend to put people's backs up with that aloof manner of his, doesn't he? I'd never have dared to speak to him if you hadn't sent him in that day to ask me about some new physio techniques. I've never forgotten that, Patty. As far as I'm concerned, you brought us together, and it would be only right and proper if you were my bridesmaid. Please, Patty?'

Patty was touched. 'Lovely of you to ask me, and of course I'd be honoured! Not that I think it's altogether justified, mind you! I'm quite sure the two of you would have got together without any help from me. But if you think I had anything to do with it — well, that's what friends are for, isn't it? . . . I've never been a bridesmaid before, it's quite a daunting prospect.'

'Not to worry. As I said, we're asking only a handful of people, so don't go buying a new dress. I shall be in a suit, and you can wear what you feel most comfortable in. Oh, dear, I'm in such a tizzy, I hardly know what I'm doing! All I can think of is being with Ronnie — all the time!'

Patty kept the smile on her face until Jane's dancing footsteps faded along the corridor, then allowed her sombre thoughts to surface. She didn't for one moment begrudge either Jane or

Ronnie their joy, but she envied them, how she envied them! Jane's last words hovered in the air. How near she, Patty, had come to being with Dane all the time, how she'd looked forward to the day when that special dream would come true! She was surrounded with happiness — from Jane, Barry, Jackie. If only some would brush off on her!

9

'May I offer my congratulations, sir?' It was Mr Simpson's first ward visit of the week without his following of medical students. Doctor Dykes, nervous as usual of facing his chief on a one-to-one basis, had conveniently remembered another appointment, and Patty and the surgeon were alone.

His stiff professional mask vanished, and his face softened into a smile. 'Thank you, Sister. Thank you for your good wishes. Thanks even more for helping me to see what — or, rather, who — was under my nose! I'd never have dared to speak to Jane if you hadn't given me that gentle prod!'

'Nonsense!' Patty warmed with inner pleasure. They'd been afraid of each other! How splendid that an idle impulse of hers had achieved the miracle. 'I'm glad for both of you that

260

everything has come out so well. Jane's very kindly asked me to be her bridesmaid, so I have a very personal interest in the wedding.'

'And are you planning your own?' It was the first time he'd ever mentioned Dane, however obliquely, since the American had visited him after his operation.

Patty's smile faded. 'Dane and I won't be seeing each other again,' she said shortly, and turned her attention to pouring coffee for them both. Mr Simpson made no comment, and his visit finished on a discussion of the condition of two post-ops, and how soon they could be considered fit for discharge.

Patty resigned herself to having to listen to wedding talk till the end of the year, and vowed not to let any of the brides-to-be get the slightest hint of her own wretchedness. Her shaky defences were further weakened the very next day, however. She and Jackie had the afternoon off, and Jackie asked her to join her for a walk. 'Must get the smell of disinfectant out of my nose,' she explained graphically over lunch, 'and Ken's on call.'

They walked briskly through suburban roads, heading for a small cafe on the outskirts of the town, passing bedraggled gardens, scuffing through crisp golden leaves stripped from the trees by an overnight storm. The air had the smell of autumn, the sad, faded scent of dying flowers, and there was a chill in the wind. A companionable silence left each to her own thoughts, and it wasn't until they were seated in cosy warmth, a pot of tea and a plate of cream cakes on the table between them, that they began to talk.

'Feel better now,' Jackie announced after a drink of tea. 'I'm going to have a meringue, even if it means the seams of my wedding dress have to be let out.'

'You seem to be the exception to the rule that brides lose weight before the wedding.'

'Ken likes me cuddly,' Jackie said

indistinctly, dealing inelegantly with a mouthful of cake. A little cream oozed from one side of her mouth and Patty leaned over to wipe it away with an expression of mock disgust.

'And I refuse to worry about the wedding. I've made all the arrangements that anyone could make, and if the cake's a disaster and the invitations miss out the date and the photographer forgets to load his camera, it's just too bad. Truth is, Patty, I'm really happy, and that seems to be the all-important thing. Wish I could say the same about you. Still *status quo* between you and Dane?'

'I told you it was all over.'

'But he loves you and you love him.'

'I know my own feelings. How can I be sure of his? There could even be another woman. I don't want to talk about it.'

'You're not a fighter, Patty, that's your problem. Now, if I were you . . . '

Patty flushed, trying to suppress a flash of anger. 'But you're not me. And

I don't need any advice, Jackie. Sorry if that sounds unfriendly, but I know nothing can alter the position, and if I can accept that, so, surely, can you.'

'Don't upset yourself, kid, I'm not about to take offence at this point in our relationship. You keep your point of view. But you can't stop me holding on to mine, which is that something should be done to get the two of you together again.'

Patty pushed back her chair, and only Jackie's hold on her arm kept her seated. 'Cool it, Patty. I understand a lot more than you give me credit for, and I shan't mention Dane again, that's a promise. OK? Still friends?'

Patty summoned up a weak smile. She was angry with herself for her reaction to her friend, and conscious of a desperate wish that someone could, indeed, do something for her. A fairy godmother, perhaps, who, at a wave of her wand, would skip over the months up to the end of Dane's year of service, and deposit him at her feet, demanding her hand in marriage. At the notion, the last of her ill humour dispersed, and they set off on the return journey with no more clouds between them.

'I suppose you know about Jane and Ronnie?'

'Saw her this morning. Great news. Not unexpected, of course.'

'Did she tell you she'd asked me to be her bridesmaid?'

'No. Lucky you! She said only that it was going to be a quiet affair. Not surprising. She hasn't any family. Don't know about him.'

'They're both rather alone in the world, I think.'

'She didn't mention a date. Do you know when it's likely to be?'

' 'Soon' is all she told me. Could be any time.'

It was, in fact, fixed for two months later, and as an important member of the wedding party, Patty found herself in the position of sounding-board as Jane consulted her on all kinds of problems, from the hymns to the honeymoon. Some of them contrived to sort themselves out.

'Remember I asked you what I should do about Paul?' Jane said one day. 'We've been so close, I didn't know how I was going to broach the subject of our going off on honeymoon and leaving him. Well, when he'd finished his lessons the other night, he said he had something to ask me.

' 'Mum,' he said, 'I know that when you and Ronnie get married you're going away on a honeymoon. Well, would you be angry if I stayed in Ronnie's house with Mrs Mac instead? You see, she said that if I stayed with her I could play with her grandchildren every day. They live quite near. There's two boys and a girl. The last time we were up at the house and you wanted a bit of peace with Ronnie, Mrs Mac showed me a little path I could go down to find them. I didn't tell you in case you'd be cross with me, but they're jolly good fun'.'

'Looks like you've found an ally in Mrs Mac.'

'She's a character, isn't she? The way she orders Ronnie about is priceless! You'd have thought she'd have been peeved when she saw us becoming so friendly, threatening her supremacy as it were, but she positively encouraged us. And, of course, she's staying on when I move in. Life will be heavenly with her to run the house for me, and she can boss me about all she likes!'

Jane spread her gladness about her, and when Patty went home on her next week-end leave, she felt, if not happy, at least less inclined to mope. A pleasant surprise was waiting for her. Gerry had started his college term and was bursting to tell her some good news.

'Now, before you say anything, Sis, I'm being very careful. Everyone knows I have to cut down on physical activities and the boys watch me like hawks to see that I don't do anything I shouldn't.

'What I want to tell you is, the principal called me up the first day and said he was glad I was able to come back and complete my course. But the most important part is that he told me the college has a special fund for giving grants of its own, and the governors had decided that as I did so well before my accident, and was probably suffering some financial strain as a result of not yet being fully fit, I was a worthy candidate!

'So you can cut down your contribution and buy some new clothes for yourself and go over to Germany or wherever and tell Dane the whole family insists that he marries you!

'I tell you, Pat, it was a blow when Mum told us about you and him. I thought, 'There go my Californian holidays. Charlie will forget me. My whole life will be blighted!' So think about it, Pat. Even if it's only for my sake and you really loathe the guy, please reconsider!'

Patty had veered from laughter to tears, and now her brother put his arms round her.

'Come on, Sis, I'm half joking, as you can guess. Don't be annoyed with me, just write my mad words off as youthful exuberance, the result of finding myself truly alive and in working order after facing a pretty grim future.'

Gerry seldom let anyone see his more serious side, and Patty stood in the circle of his arms and wept against his shoulder, not quite sure what the tears were for.

'Hey, you're soaking my shirt!' he protested. 'That's all I need — a chill, just when I'm getting into action again!'

'Oh, Gerry, I don't know what I'm bubbling about, and I'm certainly not angry with you. It's great that you're back at college and that they're giving you an extra allowance, but you can still count on my share. If you find you have something extra, put it into a savings account. You'll need it eventually for holidays or girl-friends. I don't want to hear another thing about it, and don't

269

you dare try paying me back or we'll fall out, and I shouldn't like that to happen.

'As for Dane. I'm afraid we won't be getting together. It was probably all too hasty, anyhow, and better that it should end at this stage than later, though I'm sure we'll all remember him for what he did for you — and us.'

* * *

Life levelled out for Patty over the next few weeks, with no appreciable ups or downs. In the ward every bed was kept occupied, no major emergencies cropped up, and the ever-helpful presence of Nurse Barry cushioned her from the more tiresome routines. Off duty, there was a conspiracy of silence on the subject of Dane: Jackie had been warned off, Jane knew only the bare bones of the story and discreetly avoided any mention of him, her family concentrated on welcoming her as often as she could go home.

She became conscious of an increasing lethargy, both physical and mental. She seemed to tire easily, excused herself from walking with Jackie; had no appetite, and couldn't whip up any enthusiasm for the only scheduled celebration on her calendar — Jane's wedding.

One day, despite spending her afternoon off asleep, she found the evening shift especially wearisome. The effort of doing the dressings, pushing the trolley up and down the ward, left her exhausted, and the cup of coffee she asked Nurse Henry to make for her made her feel sick.

'You all right, Patty?' Sister Cairns looked closely at her after taking the day report.

'So-so. Slight headache. Tired.'

'Hm. Watch out for the latest bug. It's already hit geriatrics.'

'I'll take something before I go to bed. So long. Hope you have a quiet night.'

The days were shortening and it was

dusk outside. Patty's feet felt leaden. She left the ward and walked laboriously along the corridor, pausing on the outside step to take a deep breath. A shadowy figure detached itself from the side of the building, and she peered at it with bleary eyes.

'Tony?'

'Absolutely.'

'Go away Tony, please. I can't cope with you just now.'

'Relax, Sister, no need to call for help. This is Tony the Repentant. Just came by to say sorry for being naughty the last time, and to tell you I've got my head of department promotion, and to thank you for everything.'

Patty looked at him, trying to register the words, shivered, felt a surge of ice through her veins and a roaring in her ears, then blackness . . .

'Hello there, Patty, are you back with us again?' She opened her eyes and stared at the masked and gowned figure in bewilderment.

'Joan Smith behind the mask, Patty.

Private wing. Everything's under control. Close your eyes and go back to sleep.' Like a child, she obeyed.

The next time she woke up she realised she'd been feverish, understood that the phantoms who had appeared at her bedside were figures out of her own dreams. Eric and Gerry had flitted by. Dane. Like a mirage he'd been conjured up out of her need for him. Even in his mask she recognised him, clutched his cool hand, told him she loved him, begged him not to leave her. Fine. So long as the touching scene had been kept to herself. How ghastly if her lovesick nattering had been overheard!

Doctor Hawkins was on duty on the wing. Elderly and white-haired, he was a fatherly figure much beloved of the older women patients. Patty had often heard about his bedside manner.

'Well, my dear, you've come to the right place for a spot of rest, we're nice and quiet up here. You've caught a nasty virus and I'm afraid you're going to be off duty for several days. But we'll make your stay as comfortable for you as we can, won't we, Sister?' She hadn't noticed Sister Smith on the other side of the bed.

Patty smiled weakly. 'Feel like a rest,' she croaked in agreement, as her eyelids came down again.

It was the third day before she was able to sit up and take some solid food.

'From what I hear, some bloke picked you up off the ground and carried you into your own ward,' the staff nurse said, taking her soup bowl away and producing a small portion of steamed fish. 'And don't make faces, Sister, you're going to have to eat everything while you're here. Doctor Hawkins calls for a detailed intake list every morning and you don't want to upset him, do you?'

'No, Nurse, of course not.' Patty giggled as she heard herself addressing a pernickety post-op patient in almost identical terms.

'I didn't — did I — was I talking my head off when I came in?' she queried, after swallowing the last spoonful of fish.

'Not that any of us noticed,' was the diplomatic answer Patty expected.

'I must have said something,' Patty persisted. 'Tell me, please, Nurse, or I'll start worrying about it and my temp will go up — and what will Doctor Hawkins say then?'

The other girl sighed. 'I always dreaded having to nurse a Sister,' she said. 'You know far too much for your own good. All right — yes, for the first couple of days you were calling for someone. I can't remember the name.'

'You can, you know,' Patty said shrewdly. 'You may as well admit it was 'Dane'.'

'Could have been. I seem to have forgotten,' was all she could get out of the nurse, and she was forced to lie back again, trying to feel thankful that as nobody knew him in the hospital, they couldn't gossip about him.

'It was that Tony Waldon who brought you in,' Nurse Barry told her when she came over to visit Patty. 'I never cared much for him, and it's a puzzle what he was doing there at that time of the evening, but he certainly did you a good turn; you might have lain there until Night Sister's visit.'

'I'm beginning to remember,' Patty said slowly, as Tony's words came back to her. 'He carried me in, I heard — hope he didn't suffer for that after his disc operation. I'm no lightweight.'

'We haven't seen him again on the ward, and if he turned up in out-patients we'd have heard about that by now.'

'I think he came to say goodbye. He left rather abruptly, I recall. How's the ward? You must be fiendishly over-worked. I can't imagine where I picked up this stupid bug, but I'm feeling a lot better so you won't be struggling on your own for much longer.'

'Everything's going along a treat. I have Nurse Barnes to lend a hand. She's third-year and good staff nurse material. You put your mind to getting your strength back. Those viruses leave their victims below par, and I don't think you've been up to the mark for a while.'

The same day a note from the CNO informed Patty that, with the concurrence of Doctor Hawkins, she was to go off the following Monday on sick leave, returning on Sunday, and, complete check-up permitting, would go back on duty the next day. It was a glorious prospect, and Patty owned, when she arrived home, that she felt just the least bit 'washed-out' — one of Mrs Henden's childhood expressions — and could do with all the cosseting her mother could give her.

The week flew, she came back, and, suddenly, Jane's wedding was only days away. Word had spread through the hospital, of course, the general consensus of opinion being that Ronnie wasn't nearly good enough for Jane, who was universally wished well, and what on earth did she see in him?

The ceremony was to be held in the

tiny church in Ronnie's village, and as Jane's guests were mainly nurses, and his guests doctors, it was to be hoped that the hospital's decimated staff weren't overwhelmed by some unexpected calamity on the day.

Mrs MacTaggart had insisted on catering for the reception, which was to be held in Ronnie's house, and was to enlist her two daughters, who lived in the village, to help with the preparations and, later, to serve the guests.

Patty had lost weight. The green dress she'd worn for that first date with Dane drooped from her shoulders, and she had to make another hole in the belt to draw it in. She fancied there were shadows under her eyes and made them up with more care than usual. The white sandals, while giving her a little more height, made her look thinner still.

Jane had arranged everything with meticulous attention to detail, and showed not a hint of nerves when Patty arrived at her home in the car ordered for her, to help her dress. She looked elegant in a dove-grey suit and tiny matching hat. She was to carry a sheaf of orchids, shading from palest pink to deep crimson. 'From Ronnie,' she said proudly. 'And these are for you.'

Patty had orchids, too, in a dozen shades of lilac and purple. 'Like them?' Patty nodded wordlessly as her friend broke off a delicate flower and pinned it in her hair. Her heart was a stone in her breast, and she wondered how she could go through with the day, an onlooker at someone else's parade of happiness.

Jane had asked Doctor Hawkins to give her away, and when he arrived Patty was sent on her way to the church, with an excited Paul, pleased with the carnation for his lapel, supplied by his future stepfather. Jane and the doctor followed soon after.

'The bridegroom's arrived, I hope?' Jane asked brightly of one of the ushers. 'He hasn't chickened out?'

'The best man's done a good job.

Ronnie's been here fifteen minutes already. He's beginning to fidget, but it won't do him any harm to wait for his bride. She's well worth waiting for,' he added gallantly.

The minister looked in to see if all were ready, and went to take up his position. Patty saw his sign to the organist. *Here comes the bride* thundered out, and Jane turned to Patty in sudden panic. 'Everything's OK,' Patty whispered in her ear, kissing her reassuringly, 'Ronnie's waiting for you.'

The church was so small, the walk to the altar took only a couple of minutes, but to Patty, eyes fixed on the back of Jane's head, it was unending. When they reached the groom, standing like a pale statue, Doctor Hawkins stepped aside to give Ronnie his place, Jane turned to hand Patty her bouquet, and the music died away. The minister cleared his throat, and began the service, 'Dearly beloved . . .'

At that moment a shaft of autumn sunshine cut through a yellow pane in one of the stained-glass windows and alighted on the best man, haloing his head and gilding his hair. Patty's eyes were unwittingly drawn to him, and she froze.

It was Dane. Dane, almost unrecognisable in a dark lounge suit. Dane, his eyes compellingly on her, holding her gaze for what seemed infinity. Dane! Why Dane? Why not? He and Ronnie had known each other for years. Dane! Why had no one told her, warned her? Why hadn't she asked Jane who the best man was to be? She'd been too selfishly wrapped up in her own misery, that was why. She'd taken it for granted Ronnie would choose one of the doctors. Dane . . . here . . .

She heard nothing of the ceremony, and realised where she was only when Dane took her cold hand and drew her into the vestry behind the newly-married couple to sign the register; tucked her arm under his as they made the return journey; held her tightly to him as they shared in the general congratulations, and finally put her into the car taking them to the reception. By then she'd got a firm hold of herself, and her heart-beats had settled to normal; her mental state was another matter.

'Champagne?' Dane handed her a brimming glass. 'Drink it down, Patty, you look all in.'

She took a couple of mouthfuls, blinking away the bubbles, and felt the crowded room closing in on her. Dane put her glass on a table and shepherded her into another, smaller room, closing the door, shutting out the voices of the guests. She dropped thankfully into an armchair, and he sat down on the floor at her feet.

'You're not over that virus yet,' he observed.

'Wh — what do you know about it?'

'Quite a lot. You were still running a temperature when I got there, but in my experience words spoken in delirium can often be accepted as perfectly valid.'

'What are you talking about?' Patty felt a hot blush suffuse her face.

'Don't you remember holding my hand? Assuring me you loved me? Pleading with me to stay with you?'

She buried her face in her hands.

He knelt before her and gently put them aside. 'What are you ashamed of? I'm happy about it! It was exactly what I wanted to hear.'

'But — but how did you know I was ill?'

'Ah, that seems to have been something of a team effort. As far as I can piece it together, the Sister on the private wing told your friend Jackie that you were crying out for someone called 'Dane'. Jackie immediately went to today's bride with the sad tale, and she told her fiancé. Ronnie phoned me, and by some miracle his message reached me right away, and I got to the hospital within six hours. Could only stay for a short time, but reckoned it was a worthwhile visit! Begged the staff and all concerned to forget I'd been there!'

283

An impish grin lit up his face.

Patty was silent, her thoughts in chaos.

'And today? Was that another plot to confuse me? You keep popping up when I least expect you, and you never arrive when it's all been planned.'

'Today? My being best man, do you mean? Reckon your friends thought it would be a nice surprise for you to find yourself paired off with me!'

'Dane — I don't know what to say.'

'Let's stick to essentials. Tell me, in full consciousness, that you love me.'

'I love you — but — '

'Patty, I don't know what went wrong the last time, but whatever that 'but' refers to, we'll work it out this time, right? Look — we love each other, OK?'

She nodded happily.

'We're going to be married, wherever you wish, whenever you say the word, OK?'

She nodded again, and he stood up and pulled her to her feet. 'Nothing else in the world matters,' he murmured hoarsely, and she responded to his kiss with a fervour that rose from somewhere inside her where her passion for him had been so unsuccessfully buried away. The orchid in her hair fell to the floor unnoticed.

'You're far too thin,' he said, caressing her body, his touch assuring her that he would give her all his love. Nothing else — nobody else mattered, indeed. Heidi fluttered briefly through her mind, to be quickly dismissed — he wasn't going to marry her, was he? He'd wait until her promise to Gerry had been fulfilled, and she'd be able to go to him in the knowledge that she hadn't let her brother down.

They tried not to stare, but Patty felt the eyes of the wedding guests turn on her and Dane as they went back into the big room, and knew they read her secret in her rapturous smile.

Jackie and Jane were quickly at her side. 'I see everything's all right. I'm so very glad,' Jane whispered.

'Here's to happy endings, Patty,' said

Jackie warmly, taking another glass of champagne from a tray proffered by one of Mrs MacTaggart's daughters, and pressing it into Patty's hand.

'Thank you.' Patty kissed them both. 'For everything. I'm so happy. And it's all due to you two.'

'A pleasure,' Jackie smiled, and Jane added, 'Isn't that what friends are for?' as they turned to be introduced to the surgeon from the USA.

THE END

We do hope that you have enjoyed reading this large print book.

Did you know that all of our titles are available for purchase?

We publish a wide range of high quality large print books including: **Romances, Mysteries, Classics, General Fiction, Non Fiction and Westerns.**

Special interest titles available in large print are:
The Little Oxford Dictionary Music Book, Song Book Hymn Book, Service Book

Also available from us courtesy of Oxford University Press:
Young Readers' Dictionary (large print edition) Young Readers' Thesaurus (large print edition)

For further information or a free brochure, please contact us at: **Ulverscroft Large Print Books Ltd., The Green, Bradgate Road, Anstey, Leicester, LE7 7FU, England. Tel:** (00 44) **0116 236 4325 Fax:** (00 44) **0116 234 0205**

Other titles in the
Linford Romance Library:

CONVALESCENT HEART

Lynne Collins

They called Romily the Snow Queen, but once she had been all fire and passion, kindled into loving by a man's kiss and sure it would last a lifetime. She still believed it would, for her. It had lasted only a few months for the man who had stormed into her heart. After Greg, how could she trust any man again? So was it likely that surgeon Jake Conway could pierce the icy armour that the lovely ward sister had wrapped about her emotions?